The Trail to Love
By
Tina Susedik

Table of Contents

The Trail to Love
by
Tina Susedik
Cover design by: Enchanted Pen Designs

This is a work of fiction. The names, characters, places, and incidents are the products of the author's imagination or are used fictitiously. Any resemblance to actual events, business establishments, locales, or persons, living or dead, is entirely coincidental.

All rights reserved. No part of this publication may be reproduced, stored in a retrieval system, or transmitted in any form or by any means (electronic, mechanical, photocopying, recording, or otherwise) without the prior consent of the author. The only exception is brief quotations in printed reviews.

The scanning, uploading, and distribution of this book via the Internet or via any other means without the permission of the author is illegal and punishable by law. Please purchase only authorized electronic editions, and do not participate in or encourage electronic piracy of copyrighted materials.

Your support of this author's rights is appreciated.

Published in the United States of America by
Tina Susedik
Copyright © March, 2024 by Tina Susedik

SEVERAL YEARS AGO, I was part of a collective "The Soul Mate Tree," with my publisher. I recently received my rights back to the book and am re-releasing it.

It involves an old, ancient tree that appears to someone who is at their deepest, darkest part of their lives. Here is the poem Char Chaffin created:

> *I am old, I am ancient, my purpose is clear*
> *To give those who are needy a treasure so dear.*
> *They who come to my roots, touch my bark, stroke my leaves*
> *Find the soul of their lives if they but believe.*
> *When I call and you listen, your prize will be great*
> *If your heart remains open and you don't hesitate.*
> *Do you yearn? Be you lonely? Is your time yet at hand?*
> *Reach for me and I'll give to you. I'm yours to command.*
> *For your trust, for your faith, keep my secrets untold*
> *And I'll gift you forever, to have and to hold.*

A few days later, I was watching my grandkids. I told them about this new project and how I needed to figure out what I wanted to write. At that point, I had never written a western or an historical, so I mentioned it to the girls, Alli, then eleven, and Emmi, then eight.

Alli was in sixth grade and yelled out: "The Oregon Trail. You need to have your characters go from Independence, Missouri to Oregon City, Oregon." I figured they must have been studying the Oregon Trail in school for her to jump on this.

For the next few hours those two little stinkers decided on my characters, plotted the book, researched horses, dogs, and clothing – and took notes. Emmi researched clothing and found all these beautiful dresses from the 1850's. (The story is set in 1859). I had to explain to her what it was like for the people on the Oregon Trail. It only took her a few minutes to find other clothing.

Here is a note Emmi (third grade) wrote – and I'm writing it exactly as she wrote it: "Sarah's ded husband, peter Nickelson, he died of rasing and the hores nockted him of and he brock his knek." This was her idea and included her twisting her neck and making a broken neck sound. And – this is exactly how I had Sarah's husband die.

I had so much fun listening to these two create my story. I have all their handwritten notes – which I'll never, ever get rid of. At one point, I let Alli read some of the story and she said, "It reads just like a movie!" Man, I love that little girl.

The Trail to Love

May 1854

Fort Laramie, Wyoming Territory

Don't cry. Don't cry. Whatever you do, don't cry. Jack Billabard wished he could put his wide-brimmed hat back on and tug the brim lower, covering his eyes to hide from the small gathering of mourners. Hat clutched in his hand; he studied the ground at his feet. No way in hell was he going to show weakness by sobbing out his broken heart.

After all, men didn't cry. Men didn't show love or pain, not in public anyway. They buried it deep inside, like the coffin being lowered by ropes into the dark earth in the small cemetery outside the walls of Fort Laramie. The coffin bearing his wife and newly born son.

Jack burrowed his nails into his palms and dug his teeth into his bottom lip. Concentrate on the physical pain. Hide the emotion. How was he supposed to drop the first handful of dirt on the wooden box? How was he supposed to walk away without flinging himself on top of his beloved Lily and the son he never had a chance to hold?

"Sir?" The traveling minister tapped him on the arm.

He blinked back the tears he'd tried so hard to stop and took a handful of dirt from the pile alongside the gaping hole. The echo of it hitting the top of the coffin would forever echo in his mind.

"Ashes to ashes. Dust to dust," the minister intoned. "The Lord bless you and keep you and give you peace."

Jack dug his teeth into his bottom lip. For the rest of his life, he'd never know another moment of peace. Never again would he give his heart to a woman, only to have it shattered to pieces. Never again would he get a woman pregnant, only to see her suffer through childbirth and die.

Someone tugged on his elbow. "C'mon, Jack," his good friend, Casey said. "You don't need to stay here. Let's go get a drink."

With one last look at the life torn from him, Jack slapped his black hat on his head. "No. A drink is the last thing I need." If he started, he may never stop.

"Whatcha gonna do?" Casey dogged Jack's footsteps to their horses tied to a row of trees.

Jack untied Papaya's reins. "I'm heading back to my place." His heart squeezed. *My place.* Not ours anymore.

"All alone? Don'tcha want company?"

"I'm sorry, Casey. I appreciate it, but I need to be alone." Jack swung his leg over the saddle. How could a man, even if he were one of his best friends, understand the pain, the rage building inside him?

A rage he needed to release in the privacy of his two hundred acres.

AN HOUR AND A HALF later, he stopped the wagon in front of the small sod cabin and set the brake. A sob tore through him. Though small and rustic, this was the place he and Lily built together. Where their life and new family were to begin.

With intentions of only a quick rest, he released Papaya's ties from the back of the wagon, unhooked the oxen from the front, and fed and watered them. He carried Papaya's saddle to the barn and slung it over a stall wall, then went back outside. As he unloaded the supplies from the wagon, tumbleweeds slapped at his legs.

Jack pushed open the oak door and entered the dim interior. Why bother putting things away? He was going to leave anyway. He dropped the supplies on the wooden table, kicked the small handmade cradle against the fireplace, used the hand pump at the sink to fill his canteen, and took some weathered meat and biscuits from a shelf.

His packed saddlebags slung over his shoulder, and with his bedroll under his arm, he went to the barn to re-saddle Papaya. In a few minutes, rifle draped across his lap, he was headed to his hills.

JACK RODE UP AND UP, ignoring the passing scenery, his mind and heart on what he'd left behind at the cemetery. Creeks overflowed from snow run-off, splashing water on his boots and pant legs as the palomino galloped through. A lone coyote chased a herd of wild horses, their manes flowing like waterfalls. Long-eared rabbits, their coats changing from winter white to summer brown, scattered like seeds in the wind and disappeared beneath rocks.

As the elevation rose, the breeze cooled. He tugged the collar of his black duster to his ears. The snow-capped mountains loomed in the distance. He' ridden farther than he'd realized.

Papaya slowed, his sides heaving. Jack didn't want to stop, but harming his horse when they were so far from home wasn't wise, either. He rode to the flowing water, dismounted, and led her to river's edge.

Knowing he wouldn't run off, he dropped the reins to the ground then pulled off the saddle and blanket, damp from sweat. Disgusted with himself for not paying better attention to his horse's needs, he wiped him down with a dry blanket from his bedroll. Some fresh grass and clear, clean water, and the horse would be set for a while.

At this elevation, only a few scrub trees were scattered about. Un-melted snow lay in the shadows of rocks and boulders. With a grunt, he carried the saddle to the sunny side of a boulder. He picked up one of the hundreds of smaller rocks, hefted it in his hand, and threw it hard enough to wrench his shoulder. "Damn!"

Jack chose another, then another, hurling them through the air, each one punctuated with a curse word. "Damn! Damn it to hell. Why did she have to die? Why wasn't it me?"

He ignored his black wide-brimmed hat flying from his head and rolling toward the saddle. Tears coursed down his cheeks, onto his coat. Rock after rock flew, until he no longer could lift anything more than a pebble.

The anger burning through him died to a smolder.

Sinking to his knees, he slammed his fists into the ground. What would he do now?

After making sure Papaya was all right, he crawled to his saddle, pulled out a blanket, and wrapped it around his shoulders. The late afternoon sun hurt his stinging eyes.

Not caring that he hadn't eaten, nor had a fire to keep him warm, nor predators at bay, he rested his head against the saddle, pulled the collar over his ears, and slapped on his hat.

Weariness from the past few days took over, and before the sun set behind the mountains, he closed his eyes and fell into a deep sleep.

COLD SEEPED INTO HIS bones. Something warm blew across his face and ears. Jack swatted at the side of his head and peeled one gritty eye open.

"Papaya!" He pushed at the horse's nose. "Go away." Papaya continued prodding at him. "Damn horse." He rubbed his cold hands together.

In the dim light, he wasn't sure if it was morning or evening. The previous day's events came back to him. He sat up and wiped a hand over his stubbly chin. Tears burned behind his eyes.

Papaya tugged at his sleeve until the only thing he could do was stand. "Dammit, horse, leave me alone." He pushed the horse to the side. The sun rising behind the mountains from the east cast a shadow on a tree Jack swore hadn't been there the night before.

Standing at least twenty feet high, the trunk was twisted and gnarled like the arthritic hands of his grandfather. Several roots rose from the ground making it look as if it would walk away. Some of its massive branches drooped close to the ground, like arms dragging across the grass.

As the sky lightened, more of the tree was visible. Unlike the rough bark of the pines at this altitude, the tree's light brown bark was smooth. Was it the lighting, or did some of the bark actually seem golden while in other places it was rough and dark brown? The surrounding trees paled in comparison.

Jack stepped closer. Pale green, oval leaves reminded him of an elm tree, only much smaller. When the wind blew, the undersides shimmered with a silvery glow.

Had he been so distraught yesterday he'd missed the massive structure? The tree seemed to beckon, calling him to its embrace. He dipped beneath its branches.

His hand shook as he reached out to touch the trunk. The instant he came in contact, his icy fingers warmed. Then his arm. He tried to pull away, but he couldn't move.

Warmth spread through his body then settled in his aching heart. Was he hallucinating or was the tree humming? Had the tree actually whispered, "Love will come?"

A calmness settled over him and the darkness of the past few days diminished.

Between the hanging branches a person, surrounded by a foggy haze, appeared. Actually, two people. One tall, the other waist high, with a smaller version of Jack's hat on its head. Suspenders held up too-short pants over the little one's plaid shirt. A woman and a boy? They held hands, swinging them back and forth as if they hadn't a care in the world. The woman's bonnet hung down her back, her waist-length hair flowing down her back.

Was the tree showing him what Lily and his child would have been like if they'd lived? His heartbeat pounded in his ears. He swore his heart cracked. As quickly as the despair washed over him, the tree hummed again and his heart warmed and peace settled through him.

Then the woman looked over her shoulder. This wasn't Lily. The sun struck the vision. Instead of his wife's dark hair, this woman's shimmered like gold. Even from this distance, her sparkling blue eyes pierced through him.

Her smile beckoned him, and when she crooked her finger, all he could do was follow. The closer he came, the farther away they moved, until their bodies faded and nothing stood before him except the large boulder he'd slept against.

The tree. What if he touched the tree again? Relive the peace flowing through him. He pivoted on his foot, ready to run back and feel the twisted branches. What the hell? Maybe he'd lost his bearings while chasing the woman and boy. He spun in each direction. Nothing. The tree was gone. Poof. Was he losing his mind and had dreamt the whole incident?

Something light brown on the ground caught his eye. Jack picked it up, his fingers warming at its touch. Bark from the disappearing tree? Had it all been real after all? If so, then where had the woman and boy gone?

Jack retraced the steps he'd taken to follow them. Only his own impressions in the dirt showed. He was going crazy. That was it. Crazy from grief. Maybe what he needed was to get away from the land and the memories it held.

Papaya pushed against Jack's back, nearly knocking him to the ground.

"What do you think, old boy?" He ran his hand over the horse's soft nose and recalled Samuel Hunt's offer of a job from before he'd married Lily. "Should I see if Sam still needs someone to help take those crazy emigrants to Oregon?"

As if he understood what Jack was saying, Papaya bobbed his large head.

"Well, since I'm already crazy, I might as well listen to you."

After a quick breakfast of cold biscuits and hard tack, he saddled Papaya, swung onto his back, and headed back down the mountain. Back to his empty home and lonesome future.

Chapter Two

January 1858

    Independence, Missouri

Sarah Nickelson held her son behind her skirts. "You leave him alone, Peter Nickelson. You can hit me all you want, but you don't touch Tommy." Her body trembled, knowing what would come from standing up to her drunk husband.

Peter stepped closer and tried to reach around her arms. "The boy needs to learn to be a man."

"The boy has a name and is only six years old. There's plenty of time for him to learn to be a man."

And hopefully not one like his father. Self-preservation kept her from saying what she thought out loud. If she could distract Peter from taking Tommy, maybe he'd forget his scheme to have their son sing in a tavern tonight. Sing for money Peter would use to drink until he passed out, leaving Tommy to find his way home in the dark.

Since Peter had heard Tommy singing one afternoon, his pure, clear voice filling their house, he had the lame-brained idea of having him literally singing for their supper. The last thing she wanted was for Tommy to spend another night learning the ways of men and women in Independence's taverns. And with their booming town of three thousand people, there were plenty of dens of iniquity to choose from.

In a few months, the city would swell as people wishing to start a new life in the west swarmed in with wagons, oxen, horses, and families. Taverns would explode with men's last chance to get drunk, which meant more crime, fights, and guns going off. Things a young boy didn't need to experience.

Despite her disappointing marriage to Peter, she was content to stay in the two-bedroom log home she'd inherited from her parents when they'd died of the fever. Every once in a while, her husband talked of heading west to Oregon City. Lately, more often than not, she dreamed of him leaving her and Tommy alone, free from his outbursts.

"Dammit, woman, give me the boy. You're coddling him."

Behind her, Tommy whimpered against her back. "Shh, Tommy. It'll be all right." Her hand brushed against the fireplace poker. Could she hold Peter off with it? He was older, stronger, and angrier. Maybe she could reason with him. She huffed out a breath. Yeah, like that ever worked before.

The black metal was warm from the fire. "Peter, listen to me." She held the poker in the folds of her skirt. "Tommy has a cold, and singing tonight would make his voice worse. I'll doctor him the rest of today and tomorrow so he'll be ready to sing the next night. If he damages his voice, he may never be able to sing again."

Peter stepped back and ran his fingers over his balding head. "I suppose you're right." He shoved a finger in her face. "He damn well better be ready to sing night after tomorrow, or there'll be hell to pay."

Sarah held her breath as her husband slammed on his hat and yanked on his overcoat. Would he change his mind before he left?

"Don't forget your scarf and gloves. It's freezing and snowing out there." For a man in his early forties, he forgot the simplest things.

"Hell, woman. Don't tell me what to do. I'm not a six-year-old you can coddle." A blast of cold air shot into the cabin as the door slammed behind him.

"Is he gone?" Tommy's small voice broke her heart.

Now that they were alone, Sarah touched her aching cheek where Peter had hit her earlier. "Yes, he's gone. It's safe to come out."

"You lied to him, Mommy. I don't have a cold."

Tommy didn't call Peter by a name any more than Peter did him. Sad, but true. Now how to explain to him why she'd lied, when she'd been telling him forever how lying was bad. Squatting down, she took her son's hands in hers. "Did you want to go with him tonight?"

"No." Tommy stuck out his bottom lip. "I hate those places. They're loud and smoky and the ladies touch me."

Sarah's stomach lurched. They touched her son? "How do they touch you, Tommy?"

He shrugged his narrow shoulders. "They kiss my cheek and play with my hair. I hate it. I hate them."

"Do they do anything else?"

Tommy shook his head.

Thank heavens. "Now about my lying. I did it to protect you. I knew you didn't want to sing tonight. If I hadn't lied, he would have taken you."

She rose, hopefully he understood what she was talking about. Picking up a chair Peter had knocked over, she summoned up a smile for her son. "Let's eat supper and read a story. Then you can go to bed."

After Tommy was asleep, she took a clean towel, put on her coat, tied a scarf over her head, slipped on her mittens, and opened the door. Cold air took her breath away. Making sure the back door was closed tight, she stepped into their small backyard, put some snow in the towel, and held it against her throbbing cheek.

What was she going to do about Peter? Marrying so quickly after her parents' death hadn't been the wisest thing to do. When Peter had come courting when she was eighteen, promising to take care of her, he seemed like a savior. A woman on her own in a town on the edge of the wilderness was not safe.

Sarah chuckled and kicked at the snow piling up on the wooden porch. Like marrying a man twice her age turned out to be a safe thing. The minute the license was signed, he became a tyrant, not the partner she'd always dreamed of.

Had it been too much to expect a loving union like her parents had?

To her dismay, it wasn't long before she learned Peter had married her for her money and not to love and take care of her. Sarah tossed the wet towel on the porch floor. How could she have been so stupid? Except for what she managed to hide in a floorboard beneath their bed, everything her father had worked for was gone. Now Peter was using their son to pay for his booze and more than likely soiled doves.

Sarah brushed the snow from a wooden rocker and sat. In no time, the cold and damp seeped through her petticoats and skirt. She swiped at her tears. Then there were the women. In a town this size, did he really think she wouldn't find out about them?

Once, in total despair, she'd approached Peter's parents, hoping they'd put a stop to his behavior. To her shock, they blamed his behavior on her. If she were a good wife, he wouldn't need to carouse and womanize. In their eyes, the sun and moon rose on their treasured son.

Snowflakes fluttered down. In the silence of the night, their whispers made Sarah wish for simpler days when she was young and her parents were alive. A thought so piercing it hurt her heart as it ran through her mind. What if Peter never returned? Life wasn't easy for a woman on her own—especially one with children. Right now, it had to be better than life with an abusive husband.

Sarah squinted. Was there a light in the backyard, near the outhouse? Was someone out there with a lantern? A shiver ran down her spine. Was it a man searching for someone to rob? Or worse?

The light didn't move. An animal? This close to the edge of the wilderness, an occasional cougar or wolf wandered into the town searching for an easy meal. Yet the light didn't look like a predator's eyes.

Sarah stood and leaned her palms on the railing. The glow became brighter and an image of a tree appeared. She took a large piece of wood from the wood pile beside the back door. Not much for protection, but it was better than nothing.

Her boots grew wet as she trudged through the deepening snow. It *was* a tree. Something this large couldn't suddenly appear, could it? She stopped. Was it humming? Calling her name? Some unseen force appeared to call to her. Maybe Peter's slap tonight rattled her brain.

Standing at least twenty feet high, the trunk was twisted and gnarled like the rough strands of yarn she used to knit mittens, scarves, and sweaters. She stepped closer, nearly tripping on one of the several roots rising from the ground. Long branches hung to the ground similar to the weeping willow trees lining a nearby creek. Would the bark feel as smooth as it seemed? Pale green, oval leaves shimmered in the breeze, their shiny undersides reminding her of fish glimmering below the surface of the creek on a sunny day.

Dare she touch it? She pulled off her mittens and spread the drooping branches aside, her hands brushing the silvery leaves. Instantly her cold hands warmed. Heat spread through her and peace settled in her heart. Peace she hadn't felt since before her parents' deaths.

Resisting its call was impossible. With trembling fingers, she touched the smooth, light brown bark. The tree became brighter, as if the sun were rising and brightening the evening sky. Sarah closed her eyes. This had to be a dream. When she opened them, she would probably find herself buried under mounds of blankets, safe and warm in her own bed.

Instead, a shadowy man appeared. He wore a wide-brimmed dark hat similar and larger to the one Tommy wore. A long heavy overcoat blew away from his tall body, revealing slim hips and broad shoulders.

Peter?

Couldn't be. Peter was shorter and stockier.

He removed his hat and raked his fingers through hair brushing his shoulders. Thick, dark hair. A long rifle hung by his side. Definitely not

Peter. Not only was her husband bald, but he'd never touched a weapon of any kind.

Sarah's heart kicked up speed when he glanced over his shoulder. His dark brown eyes stirred something deep within her. A smile revealed twin dimples and a cleft in his chin.

Who was this man, and why did he make her feel as if everything in her world was going to be all right?

A brisk wind kicked up the snow, blinding her. When the snow settled, the man and tree were gone, leaving her standing by the outhouse, holding a piece of wood, feeling more bereft and lonelier than ever.

Just a dream. Simply a dream and wishful thinking. A tall, good-looking man was never going to come into her life to save her and Tommy. She was married to Peter and nothing was going to change. She'd made her bed and would have to sleep in it.

Chapter Three

A loud pounding woke Sarah from a dream about the mystery man. A luscious dream of warm arms, sexy body, and a loving heart. She took a moment to still the blood racing through her veins. The man had been kissing her, running his hands over her bare breasts, licking her nipples, moving lower and lower . . .

For a moment she allowed herself to enjoy the delicious shiver running through her. It had been a long time since Peter had demanded his husbandly rights. So long, she couldn't even recall when.

"Mrs. Nickelson, it's Sheriff Josiah Jones. I need to talk to you."

What trouble had Peter gotten himself into this time? Drunk? Caught with another man's wife?

Probably both.

With a disgusted snort, she pulled back the covers and swung her feet to the floor. Even through her woolen socks, the cold, wooden floor curled her toes. The air turned white with every breath she took. Darn, lost in thoughts of the mysterious tree and man, she'd forgotten to add more wood to the fireplace. Peter would beat her for sure.

Throwing a shawl over her shoulders, Sarah walked around the kitchen table, and cracked open the door, looking at the sheriff through the slit.

"Can I come in?" The tall, robust man's frown didn't bode well.

The sky was still dark. "What time is it?"

"Nearly six."

Sarah tugged her shawl tighter to her neck. "I'm not dressed, Sheriff." When he nudged the door with his foot, she had no choice but to back up and let him in.

"I'm not here on a social call, ma'am." Like a gentleman should, he removed his hat. Flecks of snow dotted his coat. "I have some bad news."

This wasn't the first time the sheriff had told her Peter was in jail for being drunk and causing problems. Probably wouldn't be the last. Sarah couldn't hold back a sigh. How much was it going to cost this time? "What did he do now?"

Josiah rubbed the back of his neck and wouldn't meet her eyes. "Um. Sarah. Ma'am. I'm sorry I have bad news. Peter was killed tonight."

Letting her shawl drop to the floor, Sarah reached behind her for a chair. Her breath whooshed as she dropped to the seat. "What? What did you say?"

The sheriff retrieved the shawl and handed it to her, then squatted before her. "I know this is a shock. Several men bet him he couldn't race down the street on Jamison Gold's stallion."

"But it's storming." She pushed her hair off her face. "And everyone knows Jamison's stallion is an evil devil.

"I know." He shook his head. "You know how those men are when they're drinking."

Of course, she knew how they were. A bunch of idiots. "What happened?"

"The horse slipped on the icy street, and Peter was thrown. I'm sorry, Sarah, he broke his neck and was killed instantly."

"Where is he?"

"Since his parents' house was the closest, we took him there. I didn't think you'd want Tommy to see him."

The sheriff stood, his cracking knees breaking through the silent house. He poked the embers in the fireplace, put in pieces of wood, then blew on the red coals until flames shot up.

Now what should she do? Going to her in-laws was about as exciting as seeing her husband's body. His parents never made any bones about disliking her. Never mind when Peter had married her, he'd gained access to a lot of money, they thought she hadn't been good enough for their precious son.

"Do you want me to take you to him?"

Guilt rushed through her. Her first thought wasn't Peter was dead, but now she and Tommy were free. Her thoughts of him never coming home didn't mean she wanted him dead. "I can't leave. Tommy's still asleep."

"There's nothing you can do for Peter now, anyway."

"I'll have to go over later, once I get Tommy dressed and fed." She stood next to Josiah at the fireplace and held out her freezing hands to the warmth springing forth.

He touched her arm. "You want me to send Mary over to watch him while you deal with his folks?"

Sarah bit her bottom lip. Everyone knew what type of people the Nickelson's were. It would be better if Tommy weren't present for the inevitable scene. "Thank you. I don't know how long I'll be at their house."

Josiah's smile lightened her heart. "I'll do even one better. I'll escort you to the Nickelson's and stay until you're ready to come home."

"You don't have to, but I'd appreciate it." She'd certainly welcome his presence to stave off her in-laws' cutting remarks.

"I'd be lying if I said I didn't know what kind of man Peter was." The sheriff looked pointedly at her cheek. "His parents aren't any better. You'll need protection."

"I appreciate it, Josiah."

"I'll bring Mary here in a few hours."

"I'll be ready."

Sarah sat in the rocker by the fireplace, resting her feet on the raised stone hearth, letting its heat seep through her cold body. Her mind swirled with thoughts and images of her life with Peter. Except for Tommy, none of it was pleasant. The next few days were going to be even worse. No doubt his folks would find some way to blame his death on her.

SARAH ENTERED THE WARM, small log house she'd lived in her entire life and hung her coat and bonnet on the wooden pegs by the front door.

Thank heavens the ordeal was over. Peter's body was now stored in the winter vault behind the jail, waiting to be buried when the snow was gone and the ground thawed.

Why couldn't he have died when it was warmer and buried right away? Now she'd have to deal with his folks again. Even though he was Peter's son, they had no use for Tommy, and thankfully, wouldn't be stopping by to see him, or demanding him to come visit.

"Mary, thank you for spending the past few days with Tommy."

"It was my pleasure, dear. Tommy is such a sweet little thing. We played in the snow. He's taking a little nap." Mary poured coffee into two cups and handed one to Sarah. "I'm looking forward to the day when my children start having babies. I miss having little ones around."

Sarah's hands shook as she accepted the cup. She sat in her favorite rocker, waving her hand to a matching chair for Mary to join her. Wrapping her hands around the cup, she rested her head against the chair's tall back.

"How did it go, dear? I hope you don't mind, Josiah shared some of the events with me."

"Then you know how awful it was." Sarah sipped from her cup. Awful didn't begin to describe the humiliation.

Mary placed her hand on Sarah's arm. "Do you want to tell me about it? Sometimes it helps to talk with another person."

"You're right, Mary. I wish Mom were here to talk to. If she was though, I wouldn't have married Peter and be in this situation."

"Josiah told me they're going to sell this house. How can they do that? Isn't it yours?"

Sarah huffed. "It was until I married Peter, then my property became his. Unknown to me he wrote a will giving everything to his parents."

If he were alive right now, she'd kill him. Strangle him with her own bare hands. Hit him with a poker. Poison his beer.

"What are you going to do?"

"They are so *kindly* allowing Tommy and me to stay here for the rest of the winter. Their suggestion, no demand, is that I leave town."

Mary frowned. "Where would you go?"

Sarah pulled a brown and tattered piece of paper from her skirt pocket. "I saw this at the store." She passed it to Mary, and bit her lip waiting for the older woman's reaction.

"Are you crazy?"

"Probably." Sarah rubbed her hand across her forehead. "Being a mail-order bride is better than any other options I have. If this flyer is to be believed, this man, Mr. Sampson, is a little older than me and looking for someone to share his life with. He even says a widow with children is fine."

"What if you get out there and find out he's short, ugly, and beats women?

Sarah shook her head. "Wouldn't be much different than what I had with Peter. At least I'd be away from my in-laws. Over the years, I've managed to hide some money from Peter, but it's not enough to buy the house back."

"Ooh, I'd love to give that woman a piece of my mind. She's such a . . . a . . ."

Sarah couldn't hold back a smile. "Witch?"

Mary refilled her cup and laughed. "That's a nice way of putting it."

And it wasn't the worst of it. Sarah couldn't mention how her father-in-law suggested she stay in the house so he could 'visit' her whenever he wanted. A shudder ran through her. Sleeping with Peter was one thing, but a man in his sixties? Just the thought made her want to throw up.

"I told them my plan, and they'll help pay for a wagon, oxen, and supplies. That's how much they want me gone. If Mr. Sampson isn't paying for the trip and he turns out to be an ogre, I'm not beholden to him for paying our way to Oregon City."

"I don't understand why they are so set in your leaving."

Sarah rose. Was that Tommy sniffling? "They believe Peter's death was my fault."

"How do they figure that?"

"If I'd been a better wife, Peter wouldn't drink so much or seek out other women."

She thought about the vision of the man by the tree. Was it a sign? Maybe this Mr. Sampson was the man at the tree.

Mary slapped her hands on the rocker arms. "Hogwash. Everyone knows Peter was a drunk before he married you."

Huh. Too bad no one had told her. When she was born, Peter had been nearly twenty. As a child she had no clue what went on in taverns. His drinking had come as a complete surprise.

Mary stood and folded Sarah into her arms. Oh, how she wished it were her mother holding her. A sob rose in Sarah's chest, threatening to explode. If she started crying now she'd never stop. Mary leaned back and smiled into Sarah's tear-filled eyes.

"There's only one thing to do."

"What's that?"

"We spend the next few months preparing for your trip out west. I'll have Josiah ask around and find out what you need. And . . ." She tapped a finger against her lips. Her eyes twinkled. "When's the last time your in-laws were here?"

What was she thinking? "Not since I married Peter."

"Wonderful." Mary clapped her hands.

"Why?"

"They don't know what furniture and belongings you have, do they?"

Sarah frowned. What was Mary getting at? "No."

"You can sell things and keep the money. They'll never know the difference." Mary tapped her lip again. "Our daughter is getting married this spring and will need to set up house. Her future husband can afford to buy your things. What do you think?"

What did she think? Besides giving her some extra funds, it would be like spitting in her in-laws' faces. With her heart feeling lighter than it had in years, she pulled Mary into another hug. "I think you're wonderful."

"Good. Now get something to start making a list. We have work to do, girl."

Chapter Four

Outside Independence, Jack stood at the beginning of the line of thirty prairie schooners, ready to look for any problems with oxen, horses, and wagons. He and another guide would go through each wagon, making sure the families were prepared for the long trek to Oregon City. Then the wagon master would call to start 'jumping off.'

The first day would be short to get everyone organized. It usually took a few days for people to figure out how to drive their wagons in an orderly manner, learn the rules of the trail, and how to set up camp at the end of the day.

He hitched his collar over his neck. Even though it was early May, the morning wind was brisk and cool. Thankfully, the April rains had stopped and the ground dried out. Driving heavy wagons through mud was not a good way to start the two-thousand-mile trip.

The worst part of going through the wagons was telling people they had to leave many of their prized belongings behind. Over the past four years, he fought and argued with couples about bringing pianos, beds, dressers, and china cabinets filled with dishes. After four trips, he knew this time would be no different.

Hell, he understood folks' desires to bring family memories and the comforts of home. They needed to understand how a lighter load was easier on the oxen pulling the wagons. The trail west was littered with discarded furniture, trunks, clothing, and extra food, not to mention the bones of oxen, mules, and horses who simply gave up and out from pulling heavy loads.

So far today, the wagons he walked past looked in pretty good shape. He'd given approval for the first wagon he inspected when one of the other guides, Horace Manny, approached.

The man made Jack's skin crawl. He never shaved, so his scraggly beard hung down his chest. Bathing, or even washing occasionally, was as rare as seeing a whale in the desert. His clothes, if he ever took them off, were so encrusted with dirt they could probably stand up on their own. Despite being able to smell the man a good distance away, Horace thought he was a ladies' man, when in reality he was a no-account son-of-a-bitch.

"Hey, Billabard." Horace spit a stream of brown chewing tobacco near Jack's boots. "Did ya hear we have a widder woman traveling with us?"

Shit. Unless she was a grandma with no teeth and hands curled with arthritis, this could be a problem. Jack strode to the next wagon, knowing Horace would follow. "You don't say." Why wasn't the man checking on the stock like he was supposed to? "Are the animals ready to go?"

"Yeah, yeah, I'll check 'em in a minute." Horace stuffed another wad of chaw in his cheek, making him look like a chipmunk's cheeks full of nuts. "I hear tell she's traveling with a young boy."

"Yeah, so?"

"You know how widder woman are."

Jack rounded on the man. "No, I don't. Why don't you explain it to me."

Horace rubbed his filthy hands together. His leering smile sent warning signals to Jack. "They're lonely. Miss havin' a man take care of their needs. Could mean some fun on this trip. Too bad about the boy, though."

It probably wouldn't be a good idea to punch the guy in the face before the trip even started. What the hell was Samuel Hunt, the trail master, thinking when he hired on Horace? In Jack's mind, the man was worthless. Sometimes, it was difficult for wagon masters to find help, so he guessed hiring Horace was a last-ditch effort to get someone. Even though the man was nasty, he was known for his hunting skills.

"What do you mean, 'too bad about the boy'?"

"You know how kids are. Always gettin' in the way. Kinda cramps a man's style, if'n you know what I mean." Horace's smile didn't reach his eyes.

He needed to halt any ideas Horace may have of doing anything to this woman and her son. "Didn't you read the rules?"

"Can't read a lick."

Jack pointed a finger at the man's chest. "Then I'll remind you what Samuel *told* us. No drinking. No swearing in front of the women folk. No stealing. And most of all no fraternizing with the women."

Horace took off his grubby hat and ran his hand down the back of his neck. "Well, now. I reckon I don't know what that frat . . . whatever you said means, so I can hardly obey it, can I?"

"It means, you leave the women alone. You don't talk to them unless they talk to you. You don't eat with them unless they ask. You don't approach their fire unless given permission. You stick with guiding and hunting. Got that?"

"Well, hell, Billabard. This is one helluava long trip. Won't be long before I get invited to the widder's wagon. She's got to be awfully lonely."

"You listen to what I said and leave her alone."

Horace folded his arms across his chest. "Or what?"

"Or you'll deal with me."

"Seems like you already have your eyes set on her."

Was the man deluded? "I haven't even met the woman, so how the hell can I set my cap for her? Just do your job and stay away from the people, especially the women."

"Whatever you say." With a wink, he slapped on his hat, hitched up his pants over his bulging stomach, and sauntered away.

Shaking his head, Jack moved to the next wagon, checked the supplies, argued with the husband to lighten the load, then moved on. As he approached the middle of the line, a woman held the hand of a small boy. She glanced over her shoulder.

Jack's heart slammed in his chest. His vision blurred. For four years he'd carried the memory of the woman and lad by the strange tree. But it had been a dream. Hadn't it?

The boy tugged on her skirt, and she bent to say something to him. Wisps of blonde hair tumbled from her bun, touching the bonnet hanging down her back. A premonition hit him like a horse's kick to the stomach. Was this the widow woman? Please don't let this be the widow woman. His legs and hands shook as he approached. Hell, he was a man, and she was simply a woman. He shouldn't be nervous to talk to a woman, should he?

With a deep sigh, he slapped the side of his leg for his dog, Avery, to follow, then pulled back his shoulders and strode over to the woman and her wagon. The only thing he could do was his job. He tipped his hat.

"Ma'am. I'm Jack Billabard. I'm here to check your supplies and equipment. Can I meet with you and your husband?"

The woman reached out her hand. She wanted to shake his? This was a first. Women didn't usually shake hands. Must be one of those progressive types. Her hand and fingers were slim, almost delicate. When she slid her palm into his hand, warmth spread up his arm.

"I'm Sarah Nickelson and this is my son, Tommy." Her face turned red. "I . . . um . . . Tommy and I are traveling alone."

Shit. She was the widow. "Where's your husband?"

"Deceased." She must have picked up on his skepticism because she added quickly, "Don't worry, I can take care of myself and my son. I'm young and strong."

"You can handle your oxen and wagon?"

Sarah nodded. "Yes. I've been practicing all spring."

The temptation to feel her muscles was overpowering. Would she hit him or scream if he did? Even though she was tall, at least 5'8 to his 6'2, she was slim. She wore a simple skirt devoid of layers of petticoat which could catch on cactus and tumbleweed. Could he convince her traveling two-thousand miles without a man for protection was not a good idea?

"And I can help my mommy," the little boy said, raising his arms to show off his muscles. "I'm strong, too."

Pain shot through his heart. His son would have been a little over four already. Would he have turned out to be as protective as Tommy?

The boy tugged on Jack's pant leg. "Hey, mister. Is that your dog?" He pointed to his Australian shepherd.

"Yup."

"I gots a dog, too."

Jack squatted before Tommy and scratched Avery behind the ears. "You do? What's his name?"

"Daisy, and she's a girl." Tommy tipped his head to the side and stared at Avery's stomach. "Is your dog a girl?"

"No, he's a boy."

"Too bad, 'cause they could be friends. Boys don't like girls." Tommy ran to the back of the wagon. "Daisy. Come here."

Jack peered up at Sarah from beneath his hat. Behind her hand, he detected a hint of a smile. His heart skipped a beat. "What do you think, Mrs. Nickelson? Should Avery and Daisy be friends?"

"By all means. As long as they don't get *too* friendly, if you get my drift."

With creaking knees, he rose. Was he wrong? Had she made a sexual innuendo? Impossible. Women didn't say things like that, did they? Anyway, his wife hadn't.

Tommy returned with a small border collie in his arms. "This is Daisy. She's my bestest friend ever."

Beside him, Avery growled, then jumped at Daisy. "Down, boy. Looks as if they won't be friends after all, Tommy." Before anyone could stop her, Daisy leapt from Tommy's arms. In the way dogs do, they sniffed, circled, then bounded off together.

"Daisy!"

Sarah grabbed Tommy's arm. "She'll come back, honey. She knows where our wagon is." She picked him up and patted his shaking back. "She loves you."

Jack had a bad feeling. "Uh, Daisy's not in heat, is she?" He realized his mistake when Tommy looked at him with red, watery eyes.

"What's in heat mean? She's not sick, is she?"

A lesser man probably would have shriveled under Sarah's glare. He was made of stronger stuff—he hoped. "No, she's not sick, son. She's . . . she's . . ."

"It just means she wants to play with other dogs. Right, Mr. Billabard?"

Okay, so maybe her raised eyebrow made him shrivel a little, but not much. "Right, Mrs. Nickelson. Since they're going on this adventure together, they want to get to know each other."

Sarah's smile made him feel better. He must have said the right thing. He slapped his gloves on his pants. "I'd better check your supplies."

Tommy disappeared into the wagon. Sarah didn't say anything, simply stood, hands folded in front of her. She didn't look any older than eighteen, let alone old enough to have a boy Tommy's age. Her plain blue blouse covered medium-sized breasts, while her small waist tapered to hips made for a man's hands. Those legs under her skirt were probably long enough to wrap around a man's . . .

His body jerked. Where the hell had those ideas come from? He hadn't been interested in a woman since his wife died. Not even a glimmer of interest, and now his body was coming to life after only a few minutes of meeting her.

"Well?" Sarah interrupted the flicker of desire washing through his body.

"Well, what?"

"If you're done looking me over, are you going to check out my supplies?"

Oh, right. He was here to do a job, not lust over a widow. "Uh, Mrs. Nickelson, are you sure you can make this trip alone?" As soon as he said the words, he knew he was in trouble. Her face turned red. She slammed her hands on her hips.

"Mr. Billabard, I can assure you I can handle those oxen. I can handle the wagon, my cow tied to the back, cooking over a fire, and anything else you can throw at me."

Jack removed his hat and ran his hand down the back of his neck. "That may be so. There are other problems a woman traveling alone may encounter."

"Like what?"

"Like men."

Sarah flattened her lips and folded her arms across her chest. "I can assure you I can take care of myself and my son. If I need any help, I'll ask the family behind me. I doubt Mr. Olson would attack me. His wife would kill him."

Biting back a smile was difficult. Sarah was right. Jed Olson, in his forties, was married with nine children. From the brief encounter he'd had with the couple, he knew them to be very much in love, his brood well behaved, and the entire family willing to help where needed. But still, there were men like Horace to consider, and with a comely widow like Sarah part of the wagon train, bad things were likely to happen.

"Let me see your hands."

Sarah frowned. "What?"

"I want to see your hands."

With a sigh, she held them out, palms upward. Below each finger and alongside her forefinger were calluses. On the palm of her left hand was an unbroken blister.

"Didn't you wear gloves when you practiced driving your team?"

"Yes, I wore gloves." She curled her fingers into her palms. "The blister is from grabbing a hot pot handle. Now if you're through analyzing me, go check my supplies."

Jack inspected the side of the wagon. Like with the dogs, he had a bad feeling.

SARAH'S INITIAL REACTION to Mr. Billabard was surprise. She'd never met him, yet he seemed familiar. The way he stood with his rifle at his side reminded her of the man by the strange tree in her dream.

When they'd clasped hands, the warmth from his skin moved up her arm, rather like when she'd touched the tree. This time she couldn't explain it away as a slap on her face or from a dream.

She was very much awake and aware of Mr. Billabard's masculinity. Something fluttered near her heart, settling in her stomach. Maybe he was right. Maybe she needed to be afraid—not of other men, but his effect on her. Like she was flying down a hill on a toboggan making a beeline for a large tree.

Mr. Billabard lifted the water barrel's lid, bringing her from her disturbing thoughts. He checked the leather box containing tools necessary for repairs.

Would Mr. Billabard agree she'd prepared well?

While she understood he was only doing his job, his comments about her inability to take care of herself were irritating.

He didn't know the hours she'd spent over the past few months learning to drive the wagon with the two beasts Tommy named Rose and Tulip. Nothing she could say convinced her son those names didn't exactly fit two male oxen nearly taller than herself.

The man had no idea the blisters, the aching arms and shoulders she suffered until her body adjusted to the physical work of handling the oxen and packing for the trip. He couldn't know how she'd sold her belongings, piece by piece. Or how her body had throbbed after days of filling barrels with meat, eggs, flour, and other things for the trip.

What she didn't dare tell him was she'd burned her hand on the pot hand while learning to cook over an open fire, something she hadn't quite perfected yet. Maybe by the end of the trip, she'd figure out how not to burn everything, including her fingers.

Before preparing for the trip, she'd poured over a guidebook written by a woman whose family had made the trek in 1850. The detailed instructions on what to bring were helpful. The woman had traveled with a family of six, so Sarah cut the amount of food and supplies by two thirds then added a little more to be on the safe side.

Without having to feed Peter, she could pack less food. She'd secured eggs in barrels of cornmeal, chosen her seasonings carefully, and packed everything in the wagon per the woman's instructions, leaving room for a small bed for her and Tommy in case they couldn't sleep outside.

She'd spent the winter sewing clothes, blankets, and making sure she and Tommy had extra shoes, boots, and hats. In the spring she stored up bags of flour, brown sugar, beans, rice, coffee, and saleratus for making bread and biscuits. Instead of using her mother's old, worn-out pots and pans, she purchased a cast-iron Dutch oven and skillet. Not that it helped her cooking over a fire any.

The only bright side was knowing the bills for everything went to her in-laws. And she had no compunction in spending as much as possible.

To add to her coffers Sarah sold her favorite rockers, beds, tables, and most of her beloved books. The black and silver stove Peter had bought her for a wedding present fetched a good price. The money was now buried in a hidden compartment beneath her bed in the wagon.

Mr. Billabard walked around the wagon, interrupting her thoughts. He checked the wheels, ties of the canopy, and stepped to the rear, patting her cow. "What's her name?"

"George." At his raised eyebrow, she went on. "I know. Strange name. After Tommy named the two oxen Rose and Tulip, he chose a boy's name for the cow."

"Cute kid."

"Mommy, catch," Tommy yelled before leaping from the end of the wagon into her arms. She staggered backward, managing not to tumble to the ground by the strength of Mr. Billabard's hands at her hips. Even through her skirts and petticoat, their heat burned her skin, traveled down her stomach, and settled in her core.

"Whoa. Easy there, Mr. Nickelson. You nearly knocked your mother over."

Tommy giggled. "I'm not Mr. Nickelson. I'm Tommy."

"Well then, Tommy. You need to be careful not to hurt your mommy."

Sarah's heart broke when her son's chin wobbled. He wiggled from her arms and stood before Mr. Billabard, his small hands at his waist.

"I wouldn't ever hurt my Mommy like my daddy did." He jabbed a finger into Jack's stomach. "I love my Mommy."

Heat rose to her face. She dared not look at the man.

Mr. Billabard rested his large hand on Tommy's narrow shoulder. "I glad to hear you love your mommy and wouldn't hurt her. No man should ever hurt a woman."

"Well, my daddy hit my mommy." Tommy stuck out his bottom lip.

Sarah scooted Tommy toward the front of the wagon. "Okay, young man. That's enough. Get the bucket so we can milk George. Mr. Billabard doesn't need to hear our problems." Gathering her courage, she finally looked up at him.

"Did your husband really hit you?"

Tears pooled in her eyes. Dammit. She thought she was done crying over Peter's treatment. While Peter's mother had sobbed and wailed at the burial, she couldn't summon one tear when his body was finally lowered into the ground. She fiddled with a rope hanging from the side of the wagon. "I don't air my dirty laundry, Mr. Billabard."

"I meant what I said. Men shouldn't hit women or children. Now let me inspect the inside of your wagon, so I can move on."

A few minutes later he re-emerged. "Everything looks fine, ma'am. You have enough food and don't have to take anything out." He tipped his hat. "Nice job."

Without another word, he walked to the next wagon, his long-legged stride taking him away from her in a matter of seconds. Darn. Why had she been so prickly with him? He seemed sincere in his comments. She shook her head. She had a feeling Jack Billabard was going to play an important role on this adventure.

Chapter Five

Jack rode among the wagons, making sure everyone was set to go. After three weeks on the trail, things were running fairly smoothly, although every morning he encountered a few who thought the rules didn't apply to them.

He couldn't figure out how anyone could sleep through the warning blare of the wake-up trumpet. Some thought sleeping late or having an extra cup of coffee more important than heading out on time. Those were the same people who then figured the wagons should move all hell bent for leather, instead of going at a steady pace, thereby saving the animals from wear and tear.

After the first ten days, those who refused to keep on schedule were moved to the end. And while there hadn't been any sign of Indians, putting the fear of them attacking from the rear was enough to get the slow ones moving.

In the early morning dusk, trails of smoke from doused campfires spiraled toward the sky. Anxious to get moving, horses, oxen, and donkeys stomped, the jangle of chains, mixed with barking dogs, parents calling to their children, and mooing of cattle at the end of the train. He wove his horse through campsites acknowledging morning greetings and letting people know they had twenty minutes before leaving. The after-scent of frying bacon made the lousy hard biscuits he'd had for breakfast pale in comparison.

It wasn't until he reached the middle of the wagons when he dismounted. No one else hired on as guides had wanted the job of rousting out and getting everyone moving. He'd volunteered, not because he enjoyed being sworn and grumbled at, but because of one wagon in particular. While he vowed he'd never be interested in another woman, there was something about Mrs. Nickelson intriguing him.

It was a chance to see her and Tommy under the guise of making sure she was ready or needed help. The woman haunted his dreams, and Horace continued to make irritating noises about the comely widow. After a talk with Samuel, Horace was sent to the end of the train each morning to work toward him. Jack simply had to make sure he made it to Sarah's wagon before the smelly bastard did.

"Dammit, Rose, move over." Even though Sarah's voice barely rose above the campground noise, he heard it anyway. She'd managed to slide up the hoop on the yoke, attach it to the wagon tongue, and put the lead string through the nose ring of one of the oxen, but the second one was proving more difficult. Dare he step in and lend a hand? Except for helping her get her wagon on the ferry to cross the Missouri River, his offers of help had gone unnoticed. If anything, Sarah Nickelson was stubborn.

Jack buried a chuckle. So, the demure Mrs. Nickelson swears. Over the past weeks, she'd surprised him. Not one word of complaint. Drove her team like she'd been doing it all her life, alternating between driving them from the high front seat of her wagon, to walking alongside them. Oxen weren't the brightest of mammals. They pretty much followed whoever was in front of them.

As far as he knew she geared them up in the morning and took care of them at night. He had a sneaking suspicion she was getting help from the Olson family. Not that it mattered.

She hadn't donned her bonnet yet. Strands of loose hair tumbled from her bun. In the dim light, the color wasn't distinct. In the sunlight, it glimmered like gold. Of course, he didn't watch her. Nope. Not at all.

During an attempt to attach the team to her wagon, her shawl slipped from her shoulders revealing a short-sleeved flowery blouse tucked into her blue skirt.

"Mornin' ma'am." She jumped, hitting her head on the yoke. "Need any help?"

She stood and slapped a hand to her chest, then rubbed the top of her head. "Mr. Billabard. Don't sneak up on a person like that."

"Sorry, ma'am." He wasn't sorry at all. Could he be faulted for following her hand and getting a view of her chest? A man had to take advantage of every opportunity he could, didn't he? "What seems to be the problem this morning?"

Rose was pushing her against Tulip, making it impossible for her to get the other ox into the yoke.

"Rose is being ornery and won't let me get Tulip ready."

"Where's Tommy?"

"He's with the Olson kids." Sarah pushed at Rose's head.

"Here, let me help."

"I don't need your help, Mr. Billabard."

He couldn't hold back a sigh. "Mrs. Nickelson, it's all right to ask for help. Hell . . ." She glared. "Heck, I've helped the burliest of men hitch up their teams. Sometimes these animals can be damn . . . darn cantankerous." Maybe appealing to her friendship with the Olson's would help. "You wouldn't want to hold up the next wagons, would you?"

Using the back of her hand, she swept hair from her forehead and closed her eyes. "I suppose not, Mr. Billabard."

"Wise decision. I'll hold Rose still, while you put the yoke on Tulip." Saying flowery names for two large, male oxen nearly hurt his tongue. He took hold of Rose's head between his hands. The ox quit moving. "Okay, now's your chance."

With a few efficient steps, Sarah had Tulip in the yoke and hitched to the wagon. "Thank you for your help." She walked beside Tulip.

The instant he released Rose's head, the ox sidestepped into his partner, knocking into Sarah, tumbling her to the ground. Tulip raised his foreleg, aiming for Sarah's head. Jack's heart lurched in his chest. He grabbed her arm and yanked her away. Missing her leg by mere inches, the ox stepped on Sarah's skirt, tearing it as she was pulled away.

"You all right?" Jack didn't miss her flinch, or the alarm in her eyes when he reached out to help her stand. Her husband must have been a real bastard. Despite the warmth running up his arm from her touch, anger and fear zinged through him. "You could have been killed!"

"Thanks to you, Mr. Billabard, I wasn't." Sarah brushed the back of her skirt then noticed the rip. "Darn it all, anyway. I don't know what is up with those two today. They've never behaved like this before."

With the danger passed and his heart retreating from his throat, he admired the tantalizing view of Sarah's bare calves below her bloomers.

Sarah tugged on her fallen stockings. "Mr. Billabard, a gentleman would avert his eyes."

Jack didn't dare admit he wasn't much of a gentleman. He picked up his hat and slapped it against his pant leg. "Sorry, ma'am."

"Hmph." With the dignity of a queen holding court, head held high, nose in the air, and ignoring his proffered hand, Sarah climbed into the wagon, not realizing she'd given him another view of her shapely calves.

Mrs. Nickelson was becoming more intriguing by the day. If he was looking for another woman to share his life, she might fit the bill. Since he wasn't, it was silly of him to want to seek her out. Without another glance, he grabbed Papaya's reins and headed to the next wagon. He did not need, nor want another woman.

SARAH WAS BONE WEARY. Her backside hurt from falling this morning and then bouncing on the wooden seat of the wagon for hours. She still hadn't come to grips with the jarring of the wagon, fording rivers, taking care of the oxen twice a day, and handling a six-year-old who had more energy than anyone deserved.

Adventure? Hah! It was torture. All the practicing she'd done before leaving didn't come close to preparing her for this torture.

The oxen pulled to the left, jerking her shoulder. Damn. She'd been fighting them since this morning. She wrapped her hands tighter around the reins. Good thing she'd packed a lot of extra gloves, since this pair was nearly worn out.

At least her cooking had improved—a little, anyway. If it weren't for Greta Olson in the wagon behind her, she and Tommy would probably have starved. She cringed at the ingredients she'd wasted trying to cook over the blasted fire. Even Daisy wouldn't eat any of her messes. Too bad she couldn't use her cooking failures for fuel instead of bison chips.

Thank heavens Greta and her brood had befriended her. Before leaving her home, it hadn't crossed her mind how the other married women on the trip would take offense to a young widow traveling alone, as if she had a disease or something. Or act like she was a painted woman out to lay with every man on the trip. Heck, other than Mr. Billabard and Greta's husband, she hadn't so much as looked at another man.

That disgusting Horace Manny didn't count. Every time he came around, her skin crawled. At least with his stench, she had fair warning of his arrival and could brace herself for his innuendos. If the man ever touched her, she'd probably throw up all over him. Not that a regurgitated meal on his clothes would be noticeable.

He was the reason she and Tommy slept in the wagon at night, instead of beneath it like most people did. The first night they'd bedded down outside, Horace had shown up asking if she needed help. Daisy had taken offense to the man, growled, and snapped at his legs until the skunk had finally run off.

Since then, Daisy slept at the back of the wagon, while Sarah and Tommy slept at the front, her small gun beside her.

"Hey, Sarah. Come down and walk with me."

Joy filled her heart when Greta called to her. One of the things she was accomplished at was navigating her way from the wagon and dropping to the ground without stopping the oxen. The first time she'd tried it, the wheels had nearly run her over. After wrapping the reins around the pole, she hiked her skirt in one hand, rested her feet on the step and jumped backward. Landing on her feet was the tricky part. She lost track of the number of times she'd fallen on her rump learning the trick.

"I don't know how you do that without breaking a leg." Greta hooked her arm through Sarah's. "My heart stops whenever one of the kids try it. Since the Jacobson's little boy was killed jumping from their moving wagon, I won't let mine do it anymore."

The women were silent as they contemplated the young boy who'd recently been run over by his family's wagon. Sarah wiped away tears. How did parents handle the pain of losing a child? She couldn't imagine how she'd go on if something happened to Tommy.

"I saw that handsome Mr. Billabard at your wagon again this morning." Greta squeezed Sarah's arm.

Sarah shrugged. "He's simply doing his job. He was at yours, too."

"Well, he didn't linger at ours."

"He didn't linger, only helped me with those lousy oxen of mine. I swear I don't know what was up with those two. They were giving me so much grief this morning, I was ready to shoot them."

Greta picked an orange flower blooming along the trail and twirled it between her fingers. "I saw him get you out of the way of their hooves."

Sarah gazed at the miles of flat land ahead of them. What was her friend getting at? She surely couldn't know how Mr. Billabard filled her dreams at night as she tossed and turned inside the stuffy wagon. Damn that lousy Horace for making her feel unsafe. "Anyone would have done the same thing."

"Including Mr. Manny?"

Sarah shuddered. "That man is repulsive. If he comes creeping into my campsite again, I just may shoot him."

Greta laughed. "Not before Mr. Billabard does. The man is smitten with you."

"Horace?"

"Unfortunately, Mr. Manny is. Actually, I meant Jack Billabard. I see the way he looks at you."

It wasn't possible. They barely spoke when he came to her wagon each morning. Yet, she couldn't deny the admiration she saw in his eyes when he'd helped her from the ground. Nor could she deny the tingles spreading through her whenever she thought of him.

"Maybe you should invite him to have supper with you."

Sarah laughed. "Are you crazy? I can't figure out why cooking over a fire is so difficult for me. I never had these problems at home with the stove." Besides, would the man even accept her offer? "He'd take one bite of my burned offering and never come to my wagon again."

Tommy ran up to her, his hands filled with orange and yellow flowers. "Here, Mommy, I picked these for you."

Sarah's heart swelled with love. She swept him into her arms and kissed his cheek.

"Aw, Mommy." He wiggled from her embrace and glanced around him. "Don't kiss me in front of the others." He took off running with Greta's children.

Her little boy was growing up. For a moment she wished she and Peter had had more children. Except, he would probably have found a way to put them to work for his drinking money, too.

Beside her, Greta sighed. "They grow up so fast. I find it hard to believe my eldest is eyeing up the young men traveling with us. It won't be long and she'll be setting up a home of her own." She swiped at a tear. "Now, back to you and Mr. Billabard."

"There is no me and Mr. Billabard."

"Oh, but there could be. You're too young to be alone."

"I like being alone." And enjoyed being in charge. A man would only take away her independence—even if that independence involved a lot of hard work.

"Jed has spent some time talking with him and says Mr. Billabard is an honorable, hard-working, and lonely man. Did you know his wife died in childbirth?"

Sarah's heart ached. "How awful. How long ago did it happen?"

"I don't know. Men don't get into details. All I know is Jed likes him, and that's saying a lot."

The wagons in front of them slowed. What was going on? Usually, they were told when they were going to ford a river or stop early. Since it wasn't even lunchtime, stopping now was unusual. Before she could grab them, Rose and Tulip stood still.

"I wonder what's happening," Greta said.

Sarah shaded her eyes. In the distance a tall figure wove his horse through people walking alongside their wagons, stopping briefly at each one. As he did, parents called to their children. Her heart flipped. Indians? Where was Tommy?

In a matter of minutes, Mr. Billabard halted beside them and tipped his hat. "Mrs. Olson. Mrs. Nickelson."

"What's wrong?" Sarah tried to keep the panic from her voice as she reached for her rifle.

"There's a large herd of bison up ahead. Those critters can be dangerous. We're asking everyone to get their children into the wagons. We don't want anyone trampled if they should decide to stampede."

He tipped his hat once more before heading down the line. Sarah frowned. Had he winked at her? Greta called to the children.

"Mommy. Mommy," Tommy said, running to her, his cheeks rosy and eyes full of excitement. "Bison. Can I go see 'em?"

Sarah brought herself back from the idea that Mr. Billabard had winked at her. "No, sweetie. We have to get into our wagons in case the bison start running. Now be a good boy and do what I say."

With a pout Tommy climbed onto the seat and inside the wagon.

"I'll come back and ride with you when I get my brood settled," Greta said.

"You don't have to."

Greta chuckled. "I want to. We're not done talking about the man who winked at you."

The wagon dipped as Sarah pulled herself onto the seat. Large, dark forms milled in the distance. Excitement rushed through her, and not because of the wink. This was their first encounter with bison.

A few minutes later, Greta's popped up on the other side of the wagon. She grunted as she dropped beside Sarah. "Everyone is safe and settled."

Behind them, Tommy talked to Daisy. The dog had been listless lately, and they were worried about her.

The wagon before them inched ahead. Sarah slapped the reins. "C'mon Rose, Tulip."

"So, back to Mr. Billabard."

"There's nothing to get back to, Greta."

"Humph. I saw the way he winked at you. The man is interested."

Heat rose from her neck to her cheeks. Sarah kept her eyes on Rose's rump. "Well, *I'm* not."

"So, you say." When the wheels hit a rut Greta grabbed the side of the seat. "When a man winks, and a woman blushes at said wink, they're both interested."

After moving only a few feet, the wagon in front of her stopped.

"Whoa, boys." So, she hadn't imagined it. No man had ever winked at her before. Did it mean what Greta was saying? It didn't matter.

What mattered right now was getting to Oregon City and marrying a complete stranger.

She needed to quit thinking about Mr. Billabard at night as she tried to fall asleep, in the morning, or all afternoon while trudging beside her wagon.

Greta smoothed out her wrinkled skirt. "I still say you should invite him for supper."

"And, what? Kill him with my cooking?" Sarah rested her elbows on her knees and let the reins go slack in her fingers.

"You're getting better, my dear. Why you haven't burned anything since . . ."

Sarah couldn't hold back a laugh. "Yesterday morning?"

"You didn't ruin anything this morning."

"That's because it's difficult to spoil apples and hardtack."

Greta slid sideways. Sarah squirmed at her stare. The woman was up to something. In many ways Greta reminded her of Mary. Willing to help and warm-hearted with a bit of spunk to make life interesting.

"How about if you invited him to supper tomorrow night. You can help me cook, then take the extra food to serve him. I can even keep Tommy."

If she rustled up the courage to ask the man to supper, she definitely wanted her son as a buffer. Her feelings for the man were something she'd never encountered before. What if she said something stupid? Worse yet, what if they had nothing to talk about? Tommy never ran out of things to say.

"I don't know, Greta. I'm not very good at talking to men." Sarah understood her friend's frown.

"Weren't you married for several years? Certainly, you talked with your husband."

"Peter wasn't much of a conversationalist."

"I get the feeling I wouldn't have liked your husband very much."

Sarah shrugged. "Most people didn't."

"Including you?"

How did one admit she hated the man she'd married? Would Greta think badly of her? Staring at the flies flitting around the oxen's ears, she sighed. Either Greta would understand and remain her friend, or she would join the other women and ignore her.

"Peter was not an easy person." Sarah glanced over her shoulder to make sure Tommy wasn't listening as she explained her life with Peter. With nothing to lose, she even included being hit. Greta patted Sarah's knee a few times, but remained silent until Sarah came to the end of her tale and Peter's death.

"Even though life isn't easy for a widow with a young child, seems to me you're better off without him."

Relief washed through Sarah. "I'm glad you understand."

"I understand all right. Jed is my second husband."

If Greta had said she could sprout wings and fly, Sarah couldn't have been more surprised. "Really?"

"Yes. I was married for a year to a man my parents chose for me. He was a mean, mean drunk. Rather like your Peter."

"What happened to him?"

"I was heavy with my first child. We came to town to get some necessities. He dropped me off at the dry goods store and headed for the nearest tavern. Being as big as an ox, I couldn't carry everything, so I waited and waited. A kind gentleman finally offered to help me. When we reached our wagon, Albert staggered from the tavern and went in a rampage, accusing me of carrying on with the man who helped me. I could barely waddle down the street let alone take on another man. After knocking me to the ground, my husband picked a fight with him, and in his drunken state, tripped on a bucket left in the street and landed on the knife he'd pulled from his coat. The blade went straight through his mean, black heart."

"Oh, Greta, how horrible. What happened to the man who helped you?"

"He's in the wagon behind us. Became a father to my oldest and the following eight." Greta wiped a stray tear from her cheek. "Best day of my life was when Jed Olson asked if he could carry my bags and offered his arm to an overweight, lumbering, pregnant woman."

Sarah shook her head. "What a lovely ending to an awful story."

"So, you see my dear, good things can come out of bad situations."

Except for both of them marrying awful men, how did Greta's story relate to her? Maybe she meant something good would come from tying the knot with Mr. Sampson. "But . . ."

"Mommy, can I get down? It's hot in here."

In the distance, the mass of black moved north away from the wagon train. "Not yet honey. Hopefully, soon. I see someone riding through the wagons." From here it looked like Mr. Billabard. Her heart skipped a beat and her stomach fluttered. As the rider stopped briefly at each wagon and came closer, she held back an oath and gripped the reins.

"Howdy, Miz Nickelson." Without taking his eyes from Sarah, making her skin crawl, Horace added, "Miz Olson."

"Mr. Manny," Greta said, her voice sharp. "What's going on? When can we start moving again?"

He tipped back his hat, then leaned on the pommel. "Well, now, it might be an hour or so. The wagon master wants to make sure the bison herd has moved far enough away so's we can shoot a few for meat and not have 'em stampede us." Still staring at Sarah, he continued. "I have to move on. I'll be back later to give you ladies a hand."

A shiver ran down Sarah's spine. The last person she needed or wanted help from was Horace. "That's not necessary. We're fine."

"Oh, but it is necessary. I understand the *needs* of widder women like you." He pointed to his chest encased in a filthy buckskin jacket. "A man like *me* can satisfy those needs."

Sarah swallowed around the bile rising in her throat. How did she convince this horrible man she wasn't interested in him? Words at his audacity didn't come.

"You move along on now, Horace Manny, and leave Mrs. Nickelson alone."

Greta's voice was one she used to toe her children into line. Sarah sincerely hoped it worked on Horace.

He tipped his hat and winked. "See you soon, Miz Nickelson."

Obviously, the man was immune to Greta's authoritative manners. Amazing how one man's wink set her heart pitter-pattering and the other scared her the daylights out of her.

"Damn man."

"Greta! I've never heard you cuss before."

Greta chuckled and glanced over her shoulder into the wagon. "Well, I do, so get used to it. I simply hold back when the kids are around. There's nothing like a good swear word to relieve tension. I only wish I could have said it to Horace. Might have shocked him into believing I mean business."

"Maybe next time he comes around, I'll let out a stream of curse words." Sarah stood, hoping to see how far away the bison herd had moved. "I'm not sure what else to do to get him to understand that if he was the last man on this prairie or the Earth, I wouldn't be interested."

"I'll have Jed and my oldest boys keep an eye out for him."

Sarah fingered the small gun hidden in the pocket of her skirt. From a distance, it wasn't much use, but if someone like Horace got too close, it would do a far bit of damage. The rifle resting under the wagon seat wouldn't be much help if he got the better of her. "Thank you, but there's no need, Greta. Tommy trand I will be all right."

"If you change your mind, let me know." After a few seconds of silence, which was a lot for Greta, she interrupted Sarah's thoughts of shooting Horace. "So, are you going to do it?"

"Do what?" She sat back on the hard seat.

"Ask Mr. Billabard to supper?"

"I probably won't see him anymore today."

Greta nudged her shoulder against Sarah's. "Then ask him in the morning when he does his rounds. You know he'll stop by."

Sarah shrugged. What if he said no? What if he said yes?

Tommy poked his head through the cloth opening. "I thinks you should ask him, Mommy."

"Ask who?"

"Ask Mr. Bard to eat with us. I likes Mr. Bard. He's nice. Not mean like Daddy."

Her heart cracking, she slid over and patted the wooden seat. "Come on out here and join us, young man." When he was safely seated between them, he leaned into her side. She wrapped her arm around him. "So, you think I should invite him to supper?"

Tommy nodded into her ribs. She released a sigh so deep, she was surprised the canvas on the wagon in front of them didn't billow out and take off into the sky. How could she fight two wise people such as Greta and her son?

"All right. I'll do it." She wasn't sure how she'd summon the courage. For Tommy's sake, she would.

Chapter Six

"Why the hell am I doing this?" Jack muttered to himself as he walked past wagons and campfires where women were cooking meals whose scents would make the fullest man's stomach wish for more. As much as he looked forward to spending time with Mrs. Nickelson, her cooking skills, or lack of them, were notorious throughout the wagon train.

On more than one occasion he'd overheard women discuss the widow's cooking. They joked about how her husband must have died from starvation or food poisoning. Or how poor Tommy would never grow to be a tall, strong man when his mother couldn't rustle up one decent meal for him.

Some of the women were glad Sarah was a lousy cook because she wouldn't be able to get her hooks into their men. After all, everyone knew what widows were like. If he heard those words one more time, he wasn't going to be responsible for his actions. The few times he'd interacted with her, she'd never once tried to entice him into her lair. Just the opposite. She barely looked at him.

His stomach rumbled as he waved to families sitting around their campfires, plates of mouth-watering food resting on their knees. The closer he came to Sarah's wagon, the more he became torn. While excited to spend more than a few minutes with her, he worried he wouldn't be able to hide his dislike of her cooking. He patted his shirt pocket where a large handkerchief resided. Maybe a few coughing fits would mask his spitting food into it. He could always drop it in someone's fire pit on the way back to his bedroll.

Tommy ran up to him as he rounded the front of their wagon. Daisy followed at a more sedate pace. Had the dog gained weight? Jack thought back to the first time he'd met the Nickelson's and their dogs had run off. Not a good sign.

"Mr. Bard. Mr. Bard." Grabbing his hand, Tommy pulled Jack toward his wagon. "You really gonna eat with us tonight?"

Something heavenly wafted past his nose. Could food smelling that good taste as bad as everyone said? Bent at the waist by the fire, Sarah stirred something in a black pot. She straightened and rubbed her lower back. Every time he saw her, he couldn't get over the feeling he'd seen her before.

"Mr. Billabard." Her smile made his heart quicken. "I'm so glad you could make it. The biscuits are done and stew nearly finished. Would you care for some coffee?"

Besides her cooking, he'd heard her coffee was like drinking the grease used on the wheels and axles. "Umm . . ."

"Don't worry, I didn't make it."

When he raised his eyebrows at her, she went on. "I know what people say about my cooking." She jammed her hands into her apron pockets. "And they're right. I'm a fairly good cook over a regular stove. For some reason preparing meals over a fire has me stumped. I'd have to say you're a brave man agreeing to eat with us with the knowledge how I could be poisoning you or at least burning the food, leaving us with nothing to eat."

Now how did a man respond to such honesty? "Umm . . ." was the only thing coming to mind.

"Greta helped me. Maybe by the time this trip is over, I'll get a handle on my outdoor culinary skills."

Tommy let go of his hand and stood by his mother. "I helped, too, Mommy. Remember I poured the flour?"

Sarah smoothed back his hair. "I remember, honey. And you did a good job, too."

Why couldn't he think of anything to say? His mind was scrambled and his tongue twisted. "Umm . . ."

Sarah's lips turned up and her eyes twinkled. "Is umm all you can say, Mr. Billabard?"

"Please call me Jack."

"I couldn't possibly do that."

"Why not? We don't hold with society's rules out here in the wilderness."

"Really?" She crossed her arms over her chest. "Then why do all those biddies in the other wagons act as if they recently left the ballroom in their finest and I'm nothing more than trash?"

Shit. So, she knew what the others said about her? How did he answer? Since he had to work with those biddies and their husbands, he couldn't very well bad-mouth them, but obviously their actions and words hurt her.

He sat on one of the low stools surrounding the fire. Plates, silverware, and cups rested on a small table dropped down from the side of the wagon. He tipped his hat on the back of his head.

"I'm sorry they're treating you poorly, Mrs. Nickelson . . ."

"If I can call you Jack, I give you permission to call me Sarah."

He nodded. "Thank you, Sarah. I think they're simply jealous."

Sarah frowned, then went back to stirring the stew. Dare he tell her it smelled ready? After years of cooking his own food, he knew when something was done.

Dropping the spoon into the pot, she glanced up at him. "Jealous? Why on Earth would they be jealous?"

"You're young, beautiful, and a widow. They're afraid you'll steal their men."

Her face turned red, and she slapped a hand to her mouth. Maybe he'd said too much.

"They think I'm going to steal their men? Simply because I'm a widow? H . . ." She eyed her son. " . . . Heck, I wouldn't want any of those men if they were the last ones on earth. Besides, I saw Mrs. Johnson stealing off with a man the other night. They're both married and not to each other."

Jack jerked his chin toward the pot. "You might want to take that off the fire, Sarah. I think it's starting to burn."

He stood. Before he could help, she grabbed the handle with her bare hand and jerked back, sending the pot toppling. Its contents spilled to the ground, soaking into the dry soil in seconds.

Sarah ran to the water tank, flipped back the lid, and used the dipper to pour water over her burned hand. "Damn. I can't do anything right."

A tear ran down her cheek. It took everything in his power to keep from wiping it away. Instead, he took her hand to assess the damage. A long, angry burn crossed from one side of her palm to the other. He filled a bowl sitting on the wagon table with water and pressed her burned hand into it.

"Keep your hand in the water. Where are your eggs and honey?"

More tears pooled in her eyes. "What? You're going to cook for us since I ruined yet another meal?" She dropped onto one of the stools. "Like Peter always said, I'm worthless."

Jack ignored her comment about being worthless. If her husband had thought she was worthless, then he must have been a real ass. "The honey and egg whites will help heal your burn."

Sarah stared at her hand. "Oh. The eggs are in the wheat barrel and honey in jars wrapped in brown fabric."

After finding the items, he knelt beside Sarah.

Tommy patted the back of her other hand. "It's okay, Mommy. Mr. Bard will fix your hand."

Jack bit back a grin. The boy sounded too much like a mother soothing her injured child. After cracking open one of the eggs, he passed the contents back and forth over a plate, then tossed the yoke in the fire. As he cupped the back of her hand in his, the desire to kiss away the burn grew. As if she knew what he was thinking, she hissed in a quick breath.

"Did I hurt you?"

"No."

When he looked into her tear-filled eyes, he saw something more than pain. Fear? Shame? Surprise? Desire? If he knew her better, he might be able to decipher her emotions.

SARAH WAS A JUMBLE of emotions. Embarrassment for ruining yet another meal and burning her hand. Tenderness for the way Tommy was comforting her as if he were the adult and she the child.

When Jack placed her hand in his as if she were made of the most delicate glass, her stomach muscles jumped, her heart stuttered, and breathing became difficult. Through the tears, she became lost in his eyes. The clatter of dishes, low humming of voices, and animals making their evening noises receded into the background. Even with Tommy beside her, it was as if she and Jack were the only ones left on the prairie.

Without breaking eye contact, he spread egg whites across her burn. Almost instantly the pain receded, leaving a dull throb, rather like the one in her lower regions of her body, a feeling new, exciting, and scary all at the same time. On top of the egg whites, he dabbed the honey. A thought came to her as she glanced at the concoction on her palm.

"All I need is some flour and we might have something to eat." Even with the soothing mixture of honey and egg whites and Jack's gentle touch, her palm ached, and not from the burn. What would his fingers feel like against her body? Would they be repulsive like Peter's or thrilling like in her dreams? Her nipples hardened.

"Do you have a clean hankie?" Jack interrupted thoughts making her over-heated.

"Tommy, could you get a handkerchief from the wagon? You know where they are." Sarah kept her eyes and thoughts away from the man kneeling before her. What would he think if he knew what was going through her mind and body? Would he think she was behaving the wanton everyone thought widows were?

"Sarah?"

Refusing to look him in the eyes for fear he would see her desire for him, she focused her attention on his chest. His broad chest and shoulders. A chest she itched to run her hands over. "What?"

"Do you believe in fate?"

"Fate?" Her body vibrated at the deep timbre of his voice.

"You know—things happening for a reason?"

Sarah shrugged. "I'm not sure what you're getting at."

"I wasn't going to work the trip this year. When one of the other men was injured, I was forced to come along. If I hadn't, I wouldn't have met you."

Fate or destiny? It didn't matter. "I'm going to get married once I reach Oregon City." Where was Tommy with the handkerchief?

Jack frowned. His grip tightened on her hand. "You are?"

"Yes. To Mr. Sampson."

"Do you love him?" He released her hand.

She rested her palm in her lap. "I don't know him. I'm a mail-order bride."

His eyebrows disappeared into his hair.

"You're going to get hitched to a stranger?"

"It's a long story." One she wasn't sure she cared to share with a man she barely knew.

"Why don't you tell me about it?"

"Here's the 'chief, Mommy."

Thank heavens for kids and their interruptions. Talking about Peter and her marriage wasn't how she'd planned to spend the night. She hadn't planned on burning supper, either—that was plainly inevitable. Jack took the cloth and wrapped it around her hand, tying a knot at the top.

Greta chose that moment to rush from her wagon. "My gracious, Sarah. Whatever did you do?"

"I was trying not to ruin supper and burned myself—and the stew." She cringed when her friend spied the spilled pot, then her wrapped hand.

With barely a nod, she turned to Jack. "We have plenty. Why don't you join us?"

His knees cracked when he rose. "I don't want to impose, Greta."

Greta laughed when his stomach growled. "Oh pish-posh. With Sarah's help, there's plenty for everyone."

Tommy yanked on Jack's shirt. "Please Mr. Bard. We eat with them lots because Mommy doesn't cook very well."

Heat rose to her face. Jack's eyes twinkled and his lips played into a small smile. Was he going to laugh at her? He held out his hand. Her fingers tingled when she placed them in his.

"By all means, let's join them for supper. Can I help with anything?"

Greta winked at her. "Why don't you bring the delicious rolls Sarah made. Tommy and Sarah can bring their dishes."

SARAH PLAYED WITH TOMMY'S hair as he lay across her lap. Despite her rock-hard rolls, which Jack graciously and not very convincingly said were the best he'd ever eaten, the evening passed in laughs with him regaling them with tales of his various trips across the wilderness. He seemed like such a kind, warm man. But then, so had Peter when she'd first met him.

The stories went from traveling to childhood antics. Being an only child, she reveled in the fights, games, and tribulations children in large families went through with each other. Her sides hurt from laughing.

"One time," Greta said, "one of my younger brothers was teasing me about a boy he'd overheard me say I liked. I chased him around the house with a broom and out the back door. There was a large oak tree right outside the door. He stood beneath it pointing his finger at me making kissing noises and sticking out his tongue. Right at that moment a bird, sitting on a branch above him, pooped. Said poop landed right on my brother's tongue. While he was spitting and crying, I laughed until I fell down. Since then, whenever he teases me about something, I look at him, flap my arms up and down, and tweet like a bird. Stops him every time."

After the laughter died down, the crackling fire was the only thing filling the air. Tommy lay heavy in her arms. Her neck and shoulders ached from holding him in place. Jack stood before her.

"Here, let me take him."

Not knowing how she would be able to rise from the low stool with her son's sleeping weight in her arms, she let Jack lift him. The tender way he pressed Tommy's head to his shoulder and rubbed his back in slow circles warmed her heart. It was probably the first time a male had held her son, let alone comfort him. The short distance from Greta's wagon to hers was covered much too quickly.

"For a little guy, he sure can get heavy."

Tommy leaned back in his arms. "What does bird poop taste like?"

Sarah let out an un-lady-like snort. Jack's deep chuckle rumbled through her system. Her nerve endings spiked and zapped their way to her core. The man was dangerous—physically *and* emotionally.

"I don't know young man, and I don't plan on finding out any time soon." Jack set him on the ground. "Where's his bedroll?"

"We sleep inside."

"Whatever for? It has to be a lot cooler sleeping beneath the wagon. It's only going to get warmer as we head further west."

Jack's sharp look made her squirm. Was it safe to tell him why or would he side with the skunk, Horace? "I feel safer inside."

"Safer from what? Coyotes and wolves don't come near because of all the noise. The Indians leave us alone most of the time."

Sarah nudged Tommy to the wagon. "Climb inside sweetie. I'll be there in a minute." Once he'd disappeared, she sighed. Jack wasn't going to let this go. "It's not the animals I'm afraid of. There's someone who gives me the shivers."

"Let me guess. Mr. Manny." At her nod, Jack yanked his hat from his head and slapped it against his leg. "That bastard! I'm going to have another talk with him."

"No. Don't." Sarah grabbed Jack's arm. "Greta and Jed keep an eye out for me. And if we sleep in the wagon, we'll be safe."

"I don't like this."

"Me, neither. I don't think he'll hurt me with all these people around."

Jack put his hat back on and took a step closer. "You let me know if he bothers you." He paused, leaning forward.

Was he going to kiss her? Her breath caught in her throat. Should she let him? If everyone thought she was a hussy, she might as well enjoy the reputation. She closed her eyes in anticipation, then snapped them open when he spoke again.

"I best be going. Morning will come too soon." With a tip of his hat, he strode into the evening sunset, his body a silhouette against a darkening sky.

What a fool. Thinking he was going to kiss her. She glanced around. Several women stared at her, shaking their heads as if she'd done something wrong. Busy bodies. When she smiled at each one as if they were her best friends, they ducked their heads and went about their own business.

Biddies.

Using a cloth, Sarah grabbed the handle of the blackened pot full of water she'd left sitting on the fire. It wasn't easy with only the use of one hand, but within a few minutes, she'd washed their dishes and put them back in the side storage box. She hung the pot on a hook on the side of the wagon. Tomorrow, she and Tommy would have a simple breakfast. With thoughts of possibly seeing Jack in the morning, she climbed in beside her son, thinking about the man and waiting to fall asleep.

JACK ENJOYED THE SWIRLING colors of the evening sunset as he headed to Papaya and his bedroll. Sunrises and sunsets were two of the things he enjoyed the most during these trips. So engrossed in the beauty and thinking how it didn't compare to Sarah's beauty, he barely noticed a man step from behind a rock.

"Sniffin' 'round the widder woman, Billabard?"

Shit. Horace. The last man he wanted to see when he needed to get some sleep. It wasn't his turn for night duty, so a full night's sleep was within his grasp. "What do you want, Manny?"

"I want you to stop sniffin' 'round my woman. I saw you with her tonight."

Jack tipped back his hat and planted his hands on his hips. "Your woman? Since when is Mrs. Nickelson your woman?"

Horace spat a stream of black chew, barely missing Jack's boots. The man had better stop aiming at his boots. He was tempted to take up the disgusting habit so he could spit one back at him—right in the eye.

"Since I seen her first."

Jack held back a chuckle and looked closer at Horace. His brows were turned down and lips stretched in a sneer. The man was serious. "Since when does seeing a woman first make her yours?"

"Since I said so."

"Well, now, Horace." He glanced down at this boots. "Since *I* was invited to have supper with her and her son, I guess it means she favors me over you. Has she asked *you* to join her for a meal?"

Even in the dusky light, Horace's reddened face and narrowed eyes were obvious. His fingers were clenched into his palms. Jack held back a flinch when the bounder took a step closer. Even though the man's scent made his eyes burn, he held his ground.

"She probably felt sorry for you, is all. Once she gets to know me," he pointed at his chest, "I'll be eating with her every night."

Jack rolled up on the balls of his feet. If he weren't afraid he'd lose some fingers by coming into contact with any part of Horace's body, he'd let him have it. The idea of Horace being anywhere near Sarah and Tommy was enough for his temper to erupt. "And how do you propose getting to know her better?"

Horace ran a finger beneath his nose and wiped it on his shirt. Jack's stomach rolled.

"Well, now. That's for me to know and you to find out. I'm jest tellin' you, leave my girl alone."

"And I'm telling you one more time, she's not your girl. We're to leave the women folk alone." The glint in Horace's eyes set his teeth on edge. He'd have to keep better track of the man.

"You didn't exactly leave her alone, Billabard."

What part of 'he was invited' didn't the guy get? "Like I said before, *Horace*, I was invited. Besides, we ate with the Olson's, so we weren't alone. Even if we hadn't, Tommy would have been with us, so it wasn't as if I was sniffing after her."

With a dirty look and a humph, Horace stomped off.

Keeping better care of his surroundings, Jack headed to his horse and bedroll. Dark had nearly fallen by the time he reached Papaya. He grabbed his bedroll, and instead of hunkering down right away, took it back toward Sarah's wagon. After finding a spot close enough to see if Horace would pull anything, yet far enough away not to be seen, he lay on his blanket, locked his fingers behind his neck, and stared at the stars. The long day caught up with him and in the twinkling of those stars, he was asleep.

A CREAKING SOUND SEEPED into Jack's dream. His eyes popped open, and he peered through the morning mist. Except for the persistent squeak and a few snores coming from several wagons, the camp was quiet.

Legs appeared between the slats on the other side of Sarah's rear wagon wheel. Whomever it was, and Jack had a good idea of the person's identity, squatted, then stood. A few seconds later, the person disappeared. Even though he wanted to run after the man, it would be better to wait until light to see if any damage had been done to Sarah's wagon and what, if anything could be done about it. He wouldn't let anything happen to her—not on his watch.

Chapter Seven

The blare of the morning trumpet roused Sarah with a start. Usually she woke before it sounded, but she'd struggled to sleep during the night, only to drop off as dawn approached. For some reason, every sound was amplified, and she couldn't shake the sense of someone lurking outside.

Jack's stories and laughter replayed over and over in her mind, only to be interrupted by Horace's leers and innuendos. The skunk's presence in her dreams had been so strong, she thought she'd smelled him during the night. Without waking, Daisy growled in her sleep.

"Wake up, Tommy." Sarah nudged her son, then finger-combed her long hair and twisted it into a bun. "We need to get ready and have breakfast." She straightened the small area they slept in, and after another poke in his ribs, pulled back the fabric in the front of the wagon and climbed out.

She jumped and slapped a hand to her heart. Someone knelt by the rear wheel.

"Jack." After her initial surprise at having a man squatting near her wagon, ripples of desire flickered through her. Her damn nipples hardened. Refraining from making sure her hair was in place, she stepped toward him. "What are you doing here so early in the morning?"

"To see you, of course." He rose and faced her.

Sarah's heart tripped at his comment, but she rolled her eyes at him anyway. "With all you have to do, you walked all the way down here just to see me?"

He stared at his boots. Was that a blush creeping up his neck? Why would he be blushing? And why was he here so early?

"Uh. I wanted to get a start on the day."

Something didn't quite ring true. He'd been studying her wheel. In all the mornings he'd come by, he'd never checked her wagon. Was he the one she'd sensed skulking during the night? "Is there something wrong with the wheel?"

"Uh, no." He didn't look her in the eye. "It's always good to check them occasionally to make sure they haven't come undone. With these ruts and bumps loose tires can easily happen."

Why didn't she believe him? This was the first time she'd been told to check the wheels. She'd have to ask Jed if it were something she should have been doing on a regular basis.

"Does it seem okay?"

Jack nodded, again not looking at her. "Well, I'd best get moving and let you get ready for the day." Without another word, he disappeared around the wagon.

Before she could ponder his strange actions, Tommy called to her.

"Was Mr. Bard here?"

Sarah lifted him from the wagon. She resisted the urge to cuddle him against her. Lately he was less and less inclined to snuggle. Her arms ached to hold him, keep him a little boy as long as possible. Tommy squirmed and jumped to the ground.

"How come he didn't say hi to me this morning?"

Sarah smiled. Even though he was growing up, Tommy still pouted like a baby. "I think he was in a hurry."

She stared into the morning light, searching for his tall, lanky body. The only things moving were people from other wagons going about their morning activities. "I'm sure he'll stop by later." She tapped a finger against her lip. Had he checked all the wheels, or just the one? She'd best keep an eye on the guy. Maybe he was right when he'd told her she needed to be careful with men. Now, she had to watch out for Horace *and* Jack.

Tommy tugged on Sarah's skirt. "Mommy, I'm hungry."

Sarah's heart filled with love. Thank heavens Tommy didn't look like his father, so she didn't have to be reminded daily of the man. Tommy more resembled her father, a man Sarah had always thought was quite handsome. Someday, Tommy will be a real heartbreaker. She needed to make sure he grew up to be kind and gentle to women. It would be nice for him to have a decent father figure to guide him into manhood. Hopefully, Mr. Sampson will be.

"Mommy!"

"All right." Since she'd wasted time wool-gathering, it looked as if they would be having boiled eggs, left-over, rock-hard biscuits, and dried beef for breakfast. "Get out the plates and cups for us."

Tommy frowned as he followed her instructions. "Are we having the same thing to eat again?"

"I'm afraid so."

"Can I go eat with the Olson's?"

Sarah poked him in the belly. "No, you can't go eat with the Olson's." It was a sad day when a woman's child didn't want to eat her cooking. She set the dishes on the small table and handed Tommy a bucket.

"Go milk George." Maybe if she soaked the biscuits long enough in the milk, they'd be able to chew them without losing any teeth.

SEVERAL HOURS LATER, Sarah walked alongside the oxen. They had acted up again while she hitched them up this morning. Using the whip Jed had given her, she gently swatted at their legs to keep them in line. Since it hadn't rained in a few days, the wagons traveled zig-zagged to keep from walking in clouds of dust from the wagons in front of them. While it helped, dust and dirt still covered her face, hair, and clothing. Her skin was dry, cracked, and itchy. How she longed for a long soak in a tub filled with hot water and lavender oil. The promise of stopping by a river tomorrow afternoon for bathing and washing clothes couldn't come soon enough. She had a feeling her body odor was close to Horace's.

"Sarah," Jed called from behind her. "You need to stop."

Her heart lurched in her throat. Was it Indians? More bison? Tommy was with Greta's gang. Should she call him and have him climb into the wagon? "What's wrong?"

He ran up beside her. "Your rear wheel is wobbling."

A vision of Jack squatting by it this morning ran through her mind. "Whoa, Rose. Whoa, Tulip." Since no one was directly behind her, holding up the train wasn't a problem. As she stepped to the rear, a rider galloped to her and Jed.

"There a problem, pretty lady?"

Sarah closed her eyes and groaned. "Nothing Jed and I can't handle, Mr. Manny. You best be getting back to work."

"Don't you worry, little lady," Horace dismounted. "I can fix your wheel in a jiffy."

If there was one thing she hated being called was 'little lady' as if she weren't capable of taking care of herself. At least Jed gave her some benefit for handling most everything on this trip. Fixing a wheel might prove beyond her abilities, though. Damn, why couldn't women be as strong as men?

"That's all right. Jed and I can take care of it."

Horace hitched up his pants and puffed out his chest. "Now, little lady. You need someone with muscles to wrangle that wheel into place."

Sarah slapped her hands on her hips. "First of all, Mr. Manny, I'm not your little lady. Second of all, we've told you twice we didn't need your help. And third, how did you know there was a problem with my wheel? I never said why I stopped, did I?"

Horace tipped back his hat and ran his hand over his face. "Well, now, *little lady*, I knowed what the problem was, 'cause I saw someone by the wheel early this morning." He scratched at his scruffy beard. "Looked an awful lot like that Billabard feller. Not sure what he was doin', but couldn't be nothin' good."

She glanced at Jed tightening the wheel. Why did she get the feeling Horace wasn't telling the truth? How did he know the exact time to come help? And why would either man loosen the wheel?

Jed's knees cracked when he stood. "All taken care of, Sarah."

"Why that's a right purty first name, Sarah," Horace said, eyeing her from head to foot.

The man had nerve, she'd give him that. Maybe if she were rude to him, he'd quit pestering her. "I never gave you permission to use my first name. Thank you for your offer of help, but we're ready to move on again." Without another word, she turned her back on him.

"Then I'll be seein' you around. I hear there'll be a dance tomorrow night." Horace tipped his hat. "Be sure to save me a polka."

She shuddered and ignored the creak of his saddle as he mounted. "He simply doesn't understand I'm not interested in him. I'm blamed tired of his persistence."

"He's a bad egg for sure. I'd watch out for him." Jed followed Sarah to her oxen. "Greta, the boys, and I will keep watch out, too. And I wouldn't worry about his saying Jack was sniffing around your wagon."

"I did see him kneeling by the wheel this morning."

Jed frowned. "There had to be a good reason for his being there."

"And maybe I need to be careful of both men," Sarah said, slapping Tulip's rump. Especially with how her body reacted to Jack's presence—the complete opposite of Horace's.

Sarah got the oxen moving. They'd lost too much time and were now nearly the last in line, a place she definitely didn't want to be. And getting the two oxen to move at more than a plodding pace was near to impossible. At least the Olson's would be nearby.

AFTER A BRIEF STOP for lunch and to rest the animals, Sarah forced Tommy to nap inside the wagon. The further west they traveled, the hotter it became. The boy's face was as red as the apples beginning to shrivel in the wagon. As much as she hated Missouri winters, she'd give anything for some snow or rain to cool things off a bit. How was she going to make it until they stopped at the river tomorrow?

A cloud of dust, larger than the constant wisps from the caravan, came closer. Damn, if it were Horace again, she'd have to really lay down the law. As the rider approached, she recognized the wide-brimmed hat and the man wearing it. Her breath caught, and her palms grew damp inside her gloves. He stopped alongside her and set his horse to a walk, keeping pace with the oxen.

"Howdy, Sarah." Jack's dimples deepened with his smile. "I heard you had some trouble with a wheel this morning."

They were nearly eye level. His brown eyes seemed to show concern. If he'd had a hand in loosening the wheel, why would he bring the subject up? "Yes. Jed fixed it for me."

Jack swung from his horse and took the seat beside her. The fluid movement set her heart racing. She'd never seen a man more graceful, yet masculine. Peter was lucky he could sit on a horse without nearly toppling off. Most of the time he'd been drunk, so that may have accounted for his poor horsemanship.

He took the reins from her and slapped them against the oxen's rumps. "Take your gloves off for a while and let them cool off. I can't stand wearing mine, but if I don't, I end up with rope burns."

"How far is it to the river?"

Jack chuckled. "Anxious for a swim?"

"Oh, my, yes." Sarah giggled. "I'm not sure how we can accomplish it with all the people wanting to cool off and clean up." Would the women be able to take real baths in the river? Wash their dusty hair?

"This particular river is surrounded by trees and bushes on both sides. We'll set some of the married men on either side as guards. Anyone who comes near, they'll be arrested."

"Will we be able to take actual baths with soap and everything?" Her head tingled at the thought of washing out layers of dirt and grime.

"Yes. We'll be stopping early enough in the afternoon so you womenfolk can do laundry and have it dry in time before the dance."

Dare she wear her best cream dress she'd folded so lovingly and placed in her trunk for her wedding? The blue ruffles circling the bottom, matching the long sleeves, bodice, and high neck of the top probably made the dress not the best choice for a dance on the prairie. The matching hat set the dress off to perfection. In lieu of a bouquet for the ceremony, she'd chosen a cream, frilly parasol.

With a sigh, she pushed the idea of wearing the dress to the back of her mind. It was for a wedding, not a wilderness dance. She would wear one of her everyday skirts and blouses, and not that anyone would know, her frilly pink bloomers—if she could find them. Somehow they disappeared and there was no way she could go around the camp asking if anyone had seen her under drawers.

"Would you save me a dance or two?"

Shock and a shiver of excitement raced through her. Peter hadn't been one for dancing, so it had been a long time since she high-stepped her slippers across a dance floor. "You want to dance with me?"

"Of course I do." He nudged her elbow with his. "I imagine all of the single bucks, and probably a few married ones will want to dance with a beautiful woman like you."

Heat rose to her face. How embarrassing for a woman her age to be blushing. No one had ever called her pretty, let alone beautiful. "You shouldn't say such things like that."

"Why not? If I see something beautiful, I comment on it."

"What if someone is ugly?"

Jack chuckled. "Well, now. As I see it, everyone is beautiful in his or her own way. It's all in the eye of the beholder." He maneuvered the oxen around a slower wagon. "Look at Mrs. Fitzgibbons. Why I bet she could scare away the fiercest ogre with her looks. But Mr. Fitzgibbons? Why his love for her could stretch to the moon and back." He stretched his arm to the sky. "So, he must have seen her beautiful heart and soul. If a couple is meant to be together, it doesn't matter what they look like."

Sarah nodded. "You probably shouldn't say that to me anyway. I'm going to Oregon to be married."

"What's that got to do with anything? Is this guy going to shoot me for saying you're beautiful? Has *he* ever said that to you?"

"You forget I'm a mail-order bride."

He angled his body toward her. "I still can't believe you're traveling all that way to marry someone you've never met."

"I felt I didn't have a choice. Married women with children don't have a lot of options. We aren't allowed to teach. There were no jobs for cooks or store clerks in Independence. Most of the eligible men were heading west. My last option was to become a . . ." She couldn't even contemplate becoming a soiled dove.

Jack frowned. "I never thought of it that way before."

"So, I'm heading to Oregon City to marry a Mr. Sampson."

"What if you don't come to love him?"

Was he so naïve? "Not all marriages are based on love." Hers certainly wasn't.

"Mine was."

"Can you tell me about her?"

Grim lines appeared around his mouth. He placed the reins in her lap and jumped to the ground. Grabbing the saddle horn, he swung onto his horse's back. "Maybe some other time."

With a nod in her direction, he galloped off. He must still be madly in love with her. After his reaction to her asking about his wife, he probably wouldn't even want to dance with her. How could someone compete with a dead wife? And why should she worry about it? She was in no way heading to the altar with Jack Billabard no matter how much he stirred her insides.

Chapter Eight

Jack sunk to the bottom of the river, letting the cool, refreshing water revive his weary body. Since his talk with Sarah yesterday, he couldn't get his wife or Sarah from his mind. Under the starry sky, he'd tossed and turned in his bedroll, sleep eluding him like a jackrabbit from a hungry fox.

Lily's image was getting harder and harder to visualize. Her laughter a wisp in the wind. Her soft skin and silky hair a mere memory. More and more, Sarah's features popped into his head. More and more she filled his dreams, and instead of his deceased wife, Sarah was the first person he thought of in the early morning light. So much so, he could barely contain himself from high tailing it to her campsite first thing.

He came to the surface and scrubbed the water from his face and hair. The confusion inside his heart was eating at him. He'd loved his wife. Still did. Lately his love was becoming like a butterfly. Here one moment, then flitting off the next, while he tried to catch it and hold it to his heart.

"Hey, Billabard," the wagon master called.

"Yeah, Sam?" Jack swam to the shore and grabbed a grainy bar of soap.

"You're going to shrivel up like an old granny if you stay in there much longer."

"I don't care. This water feels so damn good, I may just sleep here tonight."

"I guess then you won't mind if'n I eat your share of the vittles the ladies are putting out."

While running the soap over his body, Jack's stomach rumbled at the thought of the array of food being supplied by the women for the dance tonight. He chuckled. What would Sarah bring that anyone could actually eat? Certainly not her rolls.

There he went again. Thinking of Sarah. Lily had been a wonderful cook. The meals she could drum up from the slimmest of ingredients would have made the world's best chefs drool. Would she have been able to do the same over a campfire? According to Sarah, she didn't have any trouble cooking on a real stove. It was only campfires she struggled with.

"Besides, I saw Mrs. Nickelson all dolled up in her best bib and tucker."

"So? What does that have to do with me?" He hoped his interest in the woman wasn't obvious to everyone. Sam's next words dashed that hope.

Sam pulled on his socks. "It's as plain as the freckles on my face you've been sniffin' around her."

Shit. He didn't want people to start talking about her again. As the weeks went on, some of the women had finally warmed up to her after they came to their senses and realized she wasn't after their men. Some had even given her a few cooking tips—not that it helped any.

He stood and tossed the soap near Sam's feet. "I'm not sniffing after her. Just being friendly, is all." He let the air dry his skin before pulling on clean pants. "What are people saying about Horace? He's shown an interest in her." And if he showed any more interest, he'd give the guy a punch in the face, one which could only improve the man's looks.

"Hell. No one takes him seriously." Sam pulled his dry shirt from a nearby bush.

"He takes himself seriously enough for all of us when it comes to Sarah. You know her rear wheel was loose yesterday morning?"

"Yeah. I heard. It happens."

Jack slipped on a clean chambray shirt, the one he saved for special occasions. "What *I* think happened was that Horace had a hand in loosening it."

"Why?" Sam asked, while tugging on his boots.

"I saw someone at her wagon before the sun came up. All I was able to see were legs, so I can't be sure it was him. I thought I recognized his boots." Jack shrugged as he buttoned his shirt and tucked it into his jeans. "It's more a feeling than anything."

"I'm not sure how we can keep an eye on him, but it wouldn't be a bad idea." Sam tossed his dirty clothes over his shoulder and climbed the riverbank. "Just don't do something you'll regret."

After rinsing his dusty clothes in the river, he followed Sam's path. He'd drape them over the wheels of Sam's supply wagon. He'd keep an eye out for Horace, there was no doubt about it. Whether he'd do something to the man he'd regret, was another matter.

MEN, WOMEN, AND CHILDREN were lined up at the long tables laden down with food when Jack finally made it to the festivities. Everyone was decked out in their best, clothes buried in trunks for just such an occasion. The men wore trousers and white shirts. Foregoing their hats for the evening, most had white rims around their heads where the brims protected their faces from the sun. Polished boots would be as dusty as ever by the end of the evening.

The women did without their white aprons covering colorful skirts with ruffles around the bottoms. Some wore short-sleeved, frilly blouses tucked into their skirts. Others donned off the shoulder white tops, showing a bit of bosom. He imagined their husbands would be keeping a close eye on them.

Since tomorrow was Sunday and a day of rest and repair, tonight's festivities should be upbeat, if not wild. Anyone who imbibed too much would have a day to recuperate. While he had no problems having a drink or two, he had no intention of getting drunk. Someone had to keep an eye on the animals, two-legged and four.

During the week, even when there was music at night, drinking was frowned upon. Traveling rugged, hot, and dusty terrain while hung over didn't work well. Tonight would be an exception. Already a few of the men held mugs of what probably contained whisky or whatever liquor they'd kept hidden.

Sarah stood with Tommy at the end of the food line giving him an opportunity to observe them. With tin plate and utensils in hand, he stopped behind her, taking in the lavender scent of her skin.

Her simple, gathered, blue skirt was set off by a top with sleeves going down to her elbows. The sides of the buttoned top crisscrossed to each shoulder, showing off her smooth chest and slim neck. From his height, he imagined the edges of her breasts, not possible since they were covered. He had a good imagination. His cock twinged. Too good.

"Evening, Sarah." He reached to tip his hat, his hand waving in the air where the brim should be. He must have looked like a fool. She glanced over her shoulder, her smile sending more twinges to his groin.

"Evening, Jack." She pressed her plate to her chest and inched forward in the line. "Isn't it a glorious evening for a party? It's been so long since I've danced."

The blue sky couldn't compare to the blue of her sparkling eyes. "Why?"

"Peter didn't take much with parties and dancing, and a lady didn't attend festivities by herself." She nudged Tommy to the edge of the first table of food. "I'm not sure I even remember how."

The more he heard about her husband, the more he wanted to knock the man on his ass, if he were still alive. Why would anyone not want to take this beautiful woman to a party? He'd be proud to have Sarah on his arm, showing her off to his friends. A pang of guilt hit him. The way he'd been proud to squire Lily to gatherings—such as they were at Fort Laramie and the wilderness.

In quiet tones, Sarah urged her son to try some of the food arrayed before them. For the sake of his own stomach, he needed to ask. "What delicious dish did you make?"

Sarah's laugh sent spirals of desire through him. "Oh, my. I surely didn't make anything. Everyone agreed I'd provide the tablecloths. Pretty difficult to mess that up."

Jack fingered the corner of the red and white gingham fabric edged with swirling blue stitching. "You made these?"

Scooping up beans and plopping them on her plate, she nodded. "Sewing is the one thing I'm good at. Greta and I have come to an agreement. Tommy and I will join her family for meals, and I'll repair clothes for her gang."

"Seems like she's getting the better part of the deal." He pictured Sarah hovering over a candle at night, a mound of clothing beside her. "She's adding only two people to her meals, while you're fixing clothes for how many?"

"Eleven. Believe me, it's worth it for my son's health and well-being." She looked down at her plate. "Oh, my. I'm not sure how I'm going to be able to eat all of this."

Sarah's plate was piled as high as his, with roasted bison and chicken, potatoes, boiled eggs, beef jerky, biscuits, pie, cookies, and cake. The women had obviously been busy since stopping shortly after lunch today. She guided Tommy to a quilt spread out in the shade of a wagon. Jack glanced at his plate then the quilt. With a shrug, he followed them.

"May I join you?"

"I was hoping you would." Her smile could have melted the frosting from the cake.

"Thanks." He placed his plate next to hers. "I'll get us some coffee and water for Tommy.

Tommy piped up. "Can't I have coffee, too?"

"No, young man, you can't. It'll stump your growth."

He held back a laugh as he walked to the beverage table. It wouldn't be coffee stumping his growth, but Sarah's cooking.

Jack's eyes suddenly watered and his nostrils burned.

"Sniffin' after the wider woman again, Billabard?"

Obviously, Horace hadn't taken advantage of the river. How the hell did he think a woman would want to get within ten feet of him?

"No, Manny. She invited me to join her and Tommy."

"Maybe I'll just mosey on over there and sit a spell."

As much as he disliked the man, for his sake and everyone at the dance, the man needed to know he stunk. "Can I give you a piece of advice, Manny?"

Horace puffed out his chest. "I'm not sure you can tell me anything about wimmin that I don't already know."

"Evidently you don't know that women don't care for people who stink. And you smell worse than a skunk, bison, and badger combined. Your clothes are so dirty, they could get up and walk away on their own. You have food in your beard, and your breath is as bad as a rotten fish."

Horace raised his eyebrows. "I stink?"

"Good Lord in heaven, Manny, you smell so bad, I'm surprised people don't faint when you pass by. Nearly everyone here smells unpleasant at the end of the day. At least they wash up in the morning, powder themselves to keep fresh, and change their clothes every few days. And the men shave as often as they can."

"You think that's why Miz Nickelson isn't interested in me?"

Jack raked his fingers through his hair. Since he'd finished telling the man he stunk, dare he let him know his personality was as offensive as his body odor? Could he be so mean?

"Hell, Manny, I don't know why she's not interested in you, other than your personal habits. Who knows what goes through a woman's mind?"

"Think I should go take a dip in the river?"

"Hell, yes. And use lots of soap. And change your clothes," he added as Horace trotted away. "And burn those in the fire," he muttered. Juggling two cups in one hand and Tommy's water in the other, he headed back to Sarah.

"What did Horace want?"

"Nothing." He sat cross-legged across from her after she took the coffee from him. "I did tell him he smelled and should take a bath in the river."

"Oh, thank heavens."

"Mr. Manny stinks," Tommy said, his mouth full of meat.

"Tommy Nickelson! That's not a nice thing to say." Sarah wiped his mouth with the edge of her skirt. "And don't talk with your mouth full."

"Well, everyone says so. They laugh at him, too."

Jack contemplated Tommy's words. Dare he reprimand the boy? Even if he wasn't his son, a boy needed the guidance of a man. "It's not nice to laugh at people, Tommy." He couldn't believe he was defending the man. "Maybe Mr. Manny didn't have anyone to teach him to keep clean. Maybe he didn't have a wonderful mother like you do to teach him manners. We don't know a person's circumstances to judge them."

Tommy stopped chewing. "What's cir . . . stands?"

He didn't dare laugh after telling him people shouldn't laugh at each other. "Circumstances. It's what a person goes through in life. Maybe the things that happened to Mr. Manny in his life were bad."

"Like my daddy dying." Tommy's blue eyes widened. "But it wasn't a bad thing."

Sarah's face reddened. "Tommy. What an awful thing to say."

"Well, it's true. I didn't likes him and he didn't likes me. You're happier with him gone to heaven."

Tears pulled in Sarah's eyes. Was she happier or were those tears for the loss of her husband? He wished he knew. Maybe it was time to change the subject. "So, Tommy. I haven't seen much of Daisy lately. Where's she been?"

"She sleeps a lot." Tommy eyed his mother. "And she's getting fat."

"Fat?" He glanced at Sarah, whose face grew even redder. "Daisy is getting fat and she's sleeping?"

"I thinks you should look at her, Mr. Bard. I thinks she's sick."

Sarah coughed into her coffee cup.

"What do you think Sarah?" He couldn't help teasing. "Is Daisy sick?"

She narrowed her eyes at him. "As you probably figured out, *Mr. Billabard*, I believe Daisy is going to be a mommy."

Tommy nearly dumped his plate on the blanket. Sarah caught it just in time as her son bounced up and down. "Daisy is going to have puppies? Daisy's going to be a mommy? Oh boy, oh boy, oh boy." He paused for a second. "How did puppies get in her tummy, Mommy?"

If Sarah's face turned any redder, she'd give the coals in the fire pit a run for their money. "Yeah, Sarah, how did puppies get in Daisy's tummy?"

Sarah bit her bottom lip then looked up at him through her long lashes. "I think a man should tell a boy all about it. Don't you?"

My, she was feisty. He was never at a loss for words. He ran a hand over his face. How the hell did one tell a young boy about the birds and the bees? His heart lurched. Would his son have been as inquisitive? "Well . . ."

A harmonica's tune shrilled through the air. Saved by the music. He jumped to his feet. "Will you listen to that? It's almost time for the dance. What do you say, bud? Let's help your mother with the dishes."

Tommy pouted and crossed his arms over his narrow chest. "Don't want to."

"Hmm." Sarah tapped his nose. "That wasn't a question, Tommy, it was an order. If he can help, so can you. Then we can all get to the party sooner."

"Oh, all right." Tommy's sigh drowned out the harmonica.

"You take the silverware, and I'll take the plates. Your mommy can bring the cups. I'll race you to the river. Last one there has to dry."

Before he and Tommy had a chance to take a step, Sarah grabbed the cups with one hand and lifted her skirt with the other. In a flash she was sprinting for the river.

Why that little— "C'mon, buddy. We can't let your mother win, can we?" He swept Tommy up in his arms and chased after her laughter, realizing he hadn't felt this carefree since his wife died. He nearly dropped Tommy at the thought. He didn't want to forget Lily and his son—no matter how much he was attracted to Sarah.

SARAH STOPPED BY THE river, trying to catch her breath. She waved to several families sharing dish duty.

"That was cheating, Mrs. Nickelson." Jack said behind her. He set Tommy on the ground. "Since your mother beat us to the river, let's get our dishes washed first. Okay, little buddy?"

At Tommy's adoring look at Jack, Sarah's heart swelled with joy for her son and broke at the same time, knowing the man wouldn't be in their lives for long. While she was happy to have a man pay attention to her son, she worried he'd get too attached. When they got to Oregon City, Tommy would have to get used to yet another man, and one who might not be as nice as Jack. Maybe they needed to keep their distance from him.

"Tommy and I should do them ourselves. You can go back and join the party." Instantly she realized she'd hurt his feelings when he frowned, handed the plates to Tommy, and jammed his hands in his pockets.

"I'm sorry. That didn't come out right." She placed a hand on his forearm. He'd rolled up his sleeves to wash the dishes. The heat of his skin rushed through her like the water running over the rocks in the river. She drew her hand back as if she'd been burned. "We're used to doing for ourselves. And I can't . . ."

"Can't what?"

Oh darn, now she'd gotten herself into a pickle. "I can't get involved with another man," she managed to whisper around the lump in her throat.

"Who said anything about getting involved." He tipped his head back and looked at the sky.

For a moment she thought he wasn't going to say anything. Then he looked back at her, his brown eyes warm and tender.

"Look, I like you. I like Tommy. I think you like me. Can't we be friends?"

"Friends." She'd try hard, really hard to make the feelings growing for him whither like plants in a drought. "All right, if that's what you want."

"Hell . . . heck. It's not what I want, but what you obviously want."

When he clapped his hands, Sarah jumped.

"So, Tommy. Let's get these dishes done and get ready to kick up our heels." Turning his back to her, he squatted at the edge of the river, and with more force than necessary, cleaned their plates.

She'd really muddled things up with him. Would he still want to dance with her? Friends danced together, didn't they? She was looking forward to 'kicking up her heels' as Jack said. At least she could dance with Tommy. Which would be as much fun, wouldn't it?

She glanced at Jack's broad set of shoulders leaning into her son's much narrower set. Tommy's small hand rested on Jack's thigh. Why couldn't she have met a man like him before marrying Peter? If she had, she wouldn't have had Tommy, and she couldn't imagine life without her son.

HAVING WASHED AND RINSED their dishes, with Tommy's hand in hers, they walked back to the circle of wagons. The music grew louder. Between the harmonica, concertina, fiddles, and rapid beat on a washboard, a rousing tune of "Turkey in the Straw," greeted them. Leaving Tommy with Jack, Sarah headed to her wagon. She'd placed their dishes in the side box when a hand clasped her shoulder.

"Jack!" Not having his smell as an advanced warning, she was shocked to see Horace behind her and not Jack.

"Why you asking for him?"

Even though he'd bathed, put on clean clothing, and looked somewhat presentable, Horace still made her skin crawl, especially since he hadn't removed his hand from her shoulder.

"Let go of me, Mr. Manny." Instead of rotten fish, his breath now smelled of whiskey.

"C'mon, Sarah. I'm all clean now. That's what wimmin want, right?"

"Once again, Mr. Manny, I'm telling you to get your hand off me. And I didn't give you permission to call me Sarah."

Horace's narrowed eyes worried her. How far would he go? Everyone was at the dance. Since they were nearly the same height, she could see over his shoulder. Where were Jack and Tommy? Where were Jed and Greta? How could she appease the man?

"Not now, Mr. Manny. Tommy is waiting for me."

"What about Billabard?" He said the name as if it were a disgusting pile of oxen droppings.

"I don't know if he's waiting for me or not." She stepped around him, dislodging his hand. If she had to say she'd dance with him to get him back to the party where she was safe, then so be it. "We can't dance here, Horace. I can't hear the music well enough." His smile, which was more like a sneer, nearly had her changing her mind.

"You'll dance with me?" He stepped toward her. "How many dances?"

"You're allowed only two, Horace. You know that."

He smoothed his beard. "Two, huh? I guess that's better than none." He crooked his elbow at her.

Did he really think she was going to waltz into the group on his arm? Not a chance. She'd rather pick up dried bison chips for the entire train for the rest of the trip. "I have to finish putting away our supper things. I'll meet you there."

To her relief, Horace dropped his arm to his side. "If you say so. I'll save you a drink."

"Not likely," she muttered after he'd disappeared into the rapidly dimming sunlight. How the hell was she going to get out of dancing with him? Did he even know how to dance? Maybe she should wear iron skillets on her feet to protect her toes. At least he'd bathed and put on clean clothes. Less chance of getting lice or bugs from him.

After tossing a damp rag over the back gate, she scurried past wagons, eyeing each shadow in case Horace should jump out at her. The music and laughter grew louder as she approached the dance area outside the circle of wagons.

She hesitated and swept the grounds searching for Jack and Tommy, praying she'd find them before Horace saw her. They both stood by the table of sweets. Hopefully, Jack was curtailing the amount of cake Tommy ate, or surely the boy would end up with a tummy ache and she'd be up with him all night.

"Mommy, Mr. Bard is teaching me to dance." Tommy's awkward jumps from foot to foot put a smile on her face.

"I can see that. Will you do me the honor of the first dance?"

Tommy stomped his foot. "Mommy, a lady doesn't ask a man to dance. A man has to ask a lady."

Sarah placed her fingers on her lips to hide her grin. "I'm sorry, sir." She watched the crowd and tapped her foot, waiting for her son's request. She didn't have to wait long. Tommy tugged on her skirt.

"Ma'am?" He held out his small hand to her. "Can I . . ." He looked at Jack. "I mean, may I please get to dance with you?"

With a curtsy, she took his hand. "Why, kind sir, I thought you'd never ask." As Tommy led her to the grassy dance floor, she glanced over her shoulder. Jack's dimples deepened and his chest puffed out in what could only be described as pride. Why would someone be proud of a boy who wasn't even his own? First making Tommy help with the dishes and now teaching him how to ask a woman to dance. As much as she wished differently, he was inching his way into her heart.

By the time Sarah and Tommy had skipped and jumped their way through the lively jig, she was breathless. She'd forgotten how exhilarating dancing was, and only nine of her toes hurt. Good thing Tommy was still light or she wouldn't be walking. The look of joy on his face was worth every sore appendage. The little imp even held her hand as they walked back to Jack, who was talking with Greta and Jed.

"Here, Mr. Bard," Tommy said holding out Sarah's hand. "It's your turn now. Better ask her like you taught me or she may not dance with you."

Jack coughed into his hand and winked at Sarah. "I certainly will young man." He turned to Sarah and bowed. "Miss Sarah, may I please have the pleasure of this dance?"

Sarah couldn't hold back a giggle. First blushing like a fool and now giggling like a love-sick teenager. The man must think she was crazy. She glanced at Greta, who nodded.

"Go ahead and enjoy yourselves," Greta said. "We'll watch Tommy."

How she longed to join the merriment of the dancers to the rousing polka, but Tommy was her responsibility, not Greta's. "I couldn't possibly let you. Don't you and Jed want to dance?"

Greta flipped a hand at her. "Oh pish-posh. Jed and I are too old to dance. Besides, he couldn't get his feet going in the right direction to save his soul. The last and only time we danced, we ended up in a pile on the floor. Now shoo."

"If you say so. Thank you, Greta."

Jack put his hand at the small of her back and guided her into the crowd of partiers, weaving between flapping arms, kicking heels, and stomping feet. If this party were held in a building, surely the floor would collapse.

Her core quivered at the heat of his hand at her back. Wishing she had fancy gloves to wear as a shield between their skin, she placed her hand in his and put the other on his broad shoulder.

Before she could give any more thought to being in his arms, he pumped their arms three times to the beat of the music, then led them in an energetic polka, zigzagging through the dancers. He spun her until the faces around them blurred. His warm, deep, rich laugh vibrated through her system, making her lose the beat. Without chastising her, he stopped, pumped their arms again, and took off, barely giving her a chance to keep up with him. It seemed the man loved to dance—and was damn good at it.

The music stopped. Expecting him to lead her back to Tommy, she was surprised when he kept her in his arms and moved them to a much slower waltz. Even though he kept them at a proper distance, Sarah swore her breasts were pressed against his broad chest and their hips were joined together. She stepped on his foot. She needed to get a grip on her emotions. Maybe it was true what they said about widows—they missed being with a man. She certainly didn't miss being with Peter, and a woman could dream about being with a man like Jack.

"I'm sorry. Guess I'm better at the polka than the waltz."

Jack's brown eyes twinkled down into hers. There were those flutters going from her heart, through her stomach, and down into her female parts again. Parts lying dormant for so long, and if she was honest with herself, had never acted like this with Peter. Was something wrong with her to be reacting to a near complete stranger when she hadn't with her own husband?

"It's all right. I'm a tough guy, I can handle a dainty tromp on my toes."

"That's very honorable of you to say, but my feet aren't dainty."

Horace tapped him on the shoulder. "Cuttin' in, Billabard."

"No, you're not, Manny." Jack gripped her fingers tighter. "I'm finishing this dance with Mrs. Nickelson."

He grabbed Jack's elbow. "No, you're not. She promised me a dance, and I'm takin' it now. You can't take two dances in a row with a woman, anyway. It's . . . it's . . ." Horace stuck his nose in the air. "It's not a polite thing to do in society."

Sarah bit her bottom lip as Jack pulled away from her. The couples dancing around them gave them a wide berth. Were they expecting the men to come to blows?

"What would you know about polite society, Manny?"

"Enough to know that when a man cuts in, you have to give up the woman, Billabard."

Jack clenched his fists at his sides.

This wasn't good. "It's all right." Sarah stepped between the two men. Hopefully neither would take a swing at the other with her in the middle. "I did say I'd dance with Mr. Manny." At least the song was nearly half over.

Before Jack could argue, Horace grabbed her hand and pulled her into the mass of dancers. Even though society dictated that couples dance the waltz without touching more than their hands, Horace yanked her against his chest and ground his crotch against her pelvis.

"If you don't back off right now, Horace Manny, I'll hurt you so you won't be able to walk for a week."

"Ah, honey, this is a slow dance. A slow and ro-man-tic dance." He drew out the word romantic as if saying it that way made it so.

Sarah pushed against his chest. "I'm not your honey, nor will I ever be your honey. I agreed to dance with you to be polite. Now you be polite and hold me properly."

His whiskey-laden breath blew across her nostrils. His body may be clean, but his breath was still rancid. She turned her head away from him. Did the man just kiss her hair?

"You smell so good, Sarah. Good enough to eat."

Sarah ground her teeth before answering. Jack stood on the edge of makeshift dance floor, hands clenched into fists, his scowl fierce enough to scare away a mountain lion. How could she pacify one man who was bent on pursuing her without Jack coming to her rescue?

"Mr. Manny, how many times do I have to tell you I have not given you permission to call me by my proper name. I insist you call me Mrs. Nickelson."

Horace finally moved arms-length away and frowned. "Why can Billabard call you Sarah, and I can't?"

"Because I gave him permission to do so."

"Why him and why not me?"

How did she tell him he disgusted her with his sexual innuendos and smelly body? Besides his offensive behavior, he scared her; scared her so much that she was afraid of being alone and in a position for him to attack her.

The song finally ended, and surprisingly Horace hadn't stepped on her toes once. She tugged her hands free. "Thank you for the dance, but I need to find Tommy now."

At her son's name, Horace puckered his brow and thinned his lips. Why would her six-year-old son be a problem for him?

"Not so fast, S— Mrs. Nickelson. You gave Billabard two dances, so now I get two."

Before she could protest, he twirled her into a polka. Within a few seconds she formulated a plan. One that she hoped would keep him from wanting to dance with her the rest of the night.

"Ouch."

"Oops, sorry, Mr. Manny." She bit back a smile as she tromped on his foot. "I'm just not used to doing the polka."

Another twirl and she trounced on his other foot. Okay, so maybe that one wasn't on purpose. The way the man was stomping and attempting to twirl her around as Jack had, she couldn't keep up with his steps. By the sixth time she'd battered his feet, he stopped, making the other dancers jerk their way around them.

"You don't know how to do the polka, Mrs. Nickelson?"

"No. I'm sorry. I never had much of a chance to attend dances."

Holding onto her elbow, he limped his way to Greta and Jed. Jack and Tommy were nowhere in sight.

"I need a drink," he said over his shoulder as he scurried away.

Greta grinned. "Did you really have to step on his toes so many times, my dear?"

Heat rose up her neck to her face. "They weren't all planned. Just a few. It would have been easier to dance with a herd of bison."

"At least he'll leave you alone for the night."

Horace disappeared into the crowd of men surrounding a makeshift bar. "One can only hope." After a brief moment of relief, she turned to her friends. "Where are Tommy and Jack?"

"Tommy had to use the necessary, so Jack took him. It was a good thing he did."

"Why?"

"I suppose you couldn't see his glare, when you kept trying to keep Horace's hands off you." Greta scowled. "I believe he was ready to pound Horace into the ground."

"Umph. He has no reason to do that." Maybe if she acted naïve, Greta would drop the subject. "I was simply dancing. Nothing more, nothing less."

"I've told you before, Jack is smitten with you. Besides, it was plain enough for anyone with eyes, you enjoyed dancing with him more than with Horace." Greta tapped Sarah's forearm. "I think you're smitten with Mr. Billabard, too."

Where was Tommy when she needed him to interrupt a conversation? She stood on her tiptoes, peering over the crowd. "I'm not sure what you're talking about, Greta."

"You keep telling yourself that, my dear."

Her feelings for Jack were growing by the day. Having him hold her, even for a public dance, was like nothing she'd ever felt before. Warm, giddy, excited. Wanting him to hold her closer, maybe even steal a kiss or two. It had been so long since she'd been held, let alone kissed. Would his lips be warm? Would she feel comfort in his arms, or something more? Another thought struck her, one that brought her from her musing. What would it be like when she married a stranger?

"Mommy, mommy." Tommy grabbed her hand and jumped up and down.

Finally, the boy shows up. "What, honey?"

"We seed an eagle swoop down and catched a fish. Didn't we Mr. Bard?"

"We *saw* an eagle swoop down and *catch* a fish," Sarah corrected.

Tommy pouted and stomped his foot. "That's what I said, Mommy."

Jack put his hands on Tommy's shoulders. Sarah took in the damp bottoms of Jack's pants. Had they done more than watch the eagle when they were down by the water?

"Your mother is only correcting the way you speak, young man. So, you sound like a gentleman."

Tommy glanced up at Jack, adoration shining in his eyes. "Like you?"

Even in the dusk, Jack's blush was evident. "Well, I'd like to think I'm a gentleman."

His action toward her and Tommy proved the man was every bit a gentleman, one she approved of teaching her young son how to act. "Thank you," she mouthed at him, ignoring Greta's smug grin.

Tommy's yawn was wide enough to drive a wagon through. He leaned against her skirt.

"I believe it's time to put you to bed, young man."

"Aw, Mommy. I'm not tired."

"Yes, you are. Besides other children are going to bed, right Greta?"

"Of course they are. I saw my youngest heading to the wagon. Even though tomorrow is a day of rest, there's lots of work to be done. And big boys like you are needed to help."

Sarah took Tommy's much smaller hand in hers. "C'mon, young man." It always amazed her how one minute he was bounding all over the place and the next ready to drop where he stood.

"I'm too tired to walk, Mommy." His whine didn't bode well for the hike back to their wagon, and as big as he was getting, it was becoming more difficult to carry him. Especially when she swore he doubled in weight when he fell asleep.

"I'll carry him, Sarah."

She met his eyes. There was something in his confusing her. Desire? Was Greta right, was he interested in her? Her heart skipped a beat. Couldn't be.

Jack swung Tommy into his arms. Immediately he wrapped his arms around his neck and snuggled down. "I love you, Mr. Bard," he whispered.

Had she heard right? The only person he'd ever said that to was her. This was going to cause a huge problem when they got to Oregon City. What did Jack think?

Eyes closed, he rubbed Tommy's narrow back. His answer was so quiet, she wasn't able to catch what he said. Dare she ask? When he opened his eyes, the pain in them nearly set her back a step. Nope. Not going to ask—especially when he stepped around her.

"C'mon, Mommy," Tommy said over Jack's shoulder. "I'm tired."

The walk back to her wagon was silent as they passed smoldering fires and mothers trying to get their children settled down so they could return to the festivities. Jack set Tommy at the wagon's entrance. When he disappeared inside, Jack took her by the waist and lifted her, like she weighed nothing more than a hummingbird. Even through her skirt, her skin burned from his touch.

"I'll wait until you get him settled."

Before entering the wagon, she glanced over her shoulder. Jack leaned against the wagon, legs crossed at the ankles, arms folded over his chest, and chin tipped down. Whatever could he be thinking?

JACK WISHED HE HAD his hat so he could hide his face. The tears pooling in his eyes burned. His chest hurt trying to hold back his grief. What would Sarah think if she saw him crying?

There were times, and they were coming fewer and far between, when some little thing brought back the memories of Lily and the son he hadn't had a chance to raise. Tommy saying he loved him was one of those times. How he'd longed to hear those words from his son and missed hearing them from his wife.

When those skinny little arms wrapped around his neck, and Tommy whispered those three words in his ear, it nearly brought him to his knees. The boy had grown heavier as they walked to Sarah's wagon. He'd welcomed the weight, even though he thought his arms would fall off.

Sarah's mumbled words were too quiet to hear. Then she sang a lullaby, one Lily had sung as she'd stitched some small item of clothing for their child. He couldn't stand it. Pushing away from the wagon so hard it rocked, he stomped to the open prairie.

He tipped his head to the sky. One by one stars twinkled, almost to the beat of the polka being played in the distance, until it was as if heaven decided to send its own version of the sun. Were the stars angels sent to light up the sky? Fireflies flickered in the grass, as if they were pretending they were those stars dropped from the sky.

A distant whoop from the dance brought him back from his fanciful thinking. A hand touched his arm.

"Are you all right?" Sarah wrapped a shawl around her shoulders and eyed the sky. "I'm always amazed how much bigger everything looks out here. It's like heaven is sharing the angels with us."

His heart lurched at the words he'd been thinking. He glanced down at her. Her hair, hanging loose down her back, sparkled like diamonds in the starlight. Her alabaster skin . . . Good heavens if anyone knew what he was thinking, they'd laugh at him for his poetic ways. He was a man, not some frop writing poetry. "Is Tommy asleep?"

"Yes."

"Do you want to go back to the dance?" He hated asking, since he'd rather stay here and gaze at her beauty. Shit. There he went again.

"I told Tommy I'd stick around for a bit." She continued staring at the sky. "Besides, I believe I'm all danced out. I'd rather stay out here and enjoy the beauty of the night."

"Yeah, me, too." He tore his eyes away from her when she glanced up at him. A coyote howled in the distance, answered by another.

"Should I get a quilt so we can sit down and enjoy the night?"

With the feelings she stirred within him, it probably wasn't wise to spend any time with her, especially on a blanket. No one had ever considered him a wise man. "Sure. I'd like that."

"I'll be right back."

Even though the sun had set for the night, its rosy hue streamed across the horizon. This wasn't a good idea. He hadn't been with a woman since Lily. What if he couldn't control himself? He may not be wise, but he was a gentleman.

He wiped his palms down his pants. Was he this nervous the first time he thought about kissing Lily? He didn't think so. It had seemed to come naturally, like breathing. Maybe it was because they'd known each other most of their lives.

And he wanted to kiss Sarah. Wanted to do more than kiss Sarah. Wanted to hold her. Caress her. See if her skin was soft beneath her clothing. An ache grew in his lower regions. Hell. This hadn't happened since before Lily died. His conscience pinged. Why should he feel guilty? Lily had been gone for over four years. He was a man with a man's needs. Sarah was a beautiful woman with, he hoped, a woman's needs.

Jack raked his fingers through his hair. Hell, he wasn't any better than Manny. Well, maybe somewhat better. He'd make sure Sarah enjoyed being with him, while Horace would be bent on attacking the woman and getting what he wanted from her.

"Here we go." Sarah spread out a patchwork quilt on the ground.

Before joining her, he willed the bulge in his pants to retreat. What would she think if she saw him in this state? Probably run for her wagon and never speak to him again. Besides, he shouldn't be getting excited over another woman when he still loved his wife. Should he?

"Are you going to join me?"

After a few seconds and a deep breath, he faced her. Her eyes sparkled like dew on the grass in the morning sun. He took a step closer. Sarah worried her bottom lip. His heart slammed in his chest, and his penis pulsed.

"Sarah?"

"Jack?" Her words came out in a whisper as she shifted toward him.

One more step and he could touch her, something he'd wanted to do for some time, almost since he met her. Dare he? From the flicker of passion in Sarah's eyes, she probably wouldn't send him on his way.

Throwing caution to the wind, he cupped her cheek and ran his thumb over her skin, taking pleasure in its softness. His skin warmed like it had the night with the tree. Sarah placed her hands on his forearms. Small tremors raced through his system. She licked her bottom lip. He was lost.

If someone saw them, it was too damn bad. He needed to kiss her. Feel those full lips against his. See if they tasted as luscious as they looked.

He raised an eyebrow.

Thankfully, she read his silent question and reduced the small distance between them, her breasts touching his chest. Even through layers of clothing, he swore they burned a hole into his skin. Hiding his desire for her was now impossible.

He leaned down. As soon as his lips touched hers, his world tilted. Surely she could feel his heart slamming in his chest. Surely his erection bulging against her was obvious. He swept his tongue over her lips. Her breath puffed on his. Any second now she would certainly push him away.

SHE'D DIED AND GONE to heaven. Never had she been kissed the way Jack was kissing her. Her husband's had been dry, quick, and ineffectual. Jack's kiss was warm, wet, and overwhelming. Surely he must feel her heart pounding against him. She hooked her fingers behind his neck and held him closer.

What must he think of her? A widow, whose son slept a mere distance from them, acting like a wanton. The proper thing would be to push him away. But, oh, how she enjoyed his lips on hers, his hands cradling her cheeks. His . . . Was that . . .?

He moved his hands from her face and wrapped them around her waist, tugging her closer until her pelvis was pressed against his . . . Yes, his male member—his large male member.

His penis, or cock as Peter had called it one time when he wanted her to put it in her mouth. Her breasts flattened against his broad chest. He urged her mouth open with his tongue.

A heaviness settled in her lower regions. She needed to get closer, meld her body with his. As if they had a mind of their own, her hips swayed into his. Her legs moved apart, giving better access for his cock against her privates.

Her fingers itched to strip Jack and run them over his bare skin. Instead, she kept them hooked behind his neck, running her thumbs up and down his neck beneath his hair that had grown to his collar over the weeks.

At the beginning of her marriage, she'd been anxious, yet nervous to learn about what happened between and man and woman. Without a mother to explain things to her, she went into her wedding night not knowing what to do. Deep down she'd thought there'd be more than a quick kiss, raising of her nightgown, and him ramming into her untried body. It had been as unpleasant as plucking pin feathers from a chicken. It hurt as it did each consecutive night until she was pregnant with Tommy. Then he left her alone.

Why he'd wanted a child he didn't even call by name was beyond her. Maybe he'd been waiting for Tommy to grow up and join the drinking and carousing. And why the hell was she thinking about Peter when this handsome, amazing man was doing wonderful, new things to her body? Her skin prickled. Her nipples hardened and sent messages of pure desire through her. And all he'd done was kiss her.

Sarah moaned when he broke the kiss and tried to bring his lips back to hers. Instead, he began peppering kisses over her cheeks, eyes, and forehead. Her legs threatened to buckle beneath her when he nibbled on her earlobe. Her skin burned wherever his lips touched and hot breath brushed over her. She tipped her head to give him better access to the side of her neck.

His thigh replaced his penis against her mound. He rubbed against her until she thought she'd die from the sensations racing through her. His lips nipped beneath her chin, then caressed the chest uncovered by her top.

A scurrying nearby broke through senses being awakened by this man. Jack broke away from her, his chest rising and falling with his rapid breaths.

A tall-eared jackrabbit, chased by a coyote, darted from sagebrush to sagebrush. The coyote stopped, its body silhouetted against the night sky. Shivers ran down Sarah's spine. Shivers that had nothing to do with the coyote's appearance, but the noise she'd heard before the animals interrupted them. Something that had sounded like boots scraping and a man swearing under his breath.

Jack raked his fingers through his hair and looked down at his boots. "I'm sorry. I shouldn't have kissed you like that."

He was sorry? Well, she sure as hell wasn't. She wasn't going to let him get away with saying he was sorry.

She touched her swollen lips. "*You* may be sorry, but I'm sure not." At his raised eyebrows she went on. "I have never been kissed like that before. It's something I'll never, ever forget."

He huffed. "I'm not sorry I kissed you, Sarah. I'm sorry I kissed you in such an open place. Hell, anyone could have seen us. The women here are finally adjusting to the idea you're not after their men. If they see you and I . . ." He swept his hand out. "Doing what we were doing, then they may think you're a loose woman and will begin to ignore you again."

Sarah slapped her hands at her waist. "It's not as if you or I are married to other people. We're both single and obviously attracted to each other. What we do is none of their business."

"That's easy to say. Not easy for a woman to live through. And if any of the single men had seen us, they may think you're easy pickings."

"You mean men like Horace."

Jack pulled her into his embrace. Contentment replaced her earlier passion. How could one man create such opposing feelings in her?

He nodded against her hair. "Yes. Men like Horace."

"So, no more kissing?"

"Yes. I mean no." He stepped back, picked up the quilt, and handed it to her. "What I mean is, yes, no more kissing."

Disappointment washed through her as he escorted her back to her wagon and walked away. Damn the man. Obviously, he was attracted to her. Yet he was probably right. If word got out about what they'd done, she'd be branded a scarlet woman—even if all they did was kiss. Thinking about doing more wasn't a crime, was it?

Sarah pulled aside the white covering and disappeared inside, knowing she'd have another night of tossing and turning.

Chapter Nine

A week passed. A week of hot, dry weather, making walking nearly unbearable. A week of thinking about the night with Jack. Each night as she tried to fall asleep, she replayed those kisses over and over. Each morning when she woke after a fitful sleep, it was the first thing she thought of. All day long as she plodded alongside her oxen, trying to keep the damn things in line, her lips burned, and her female parts flared recalling his lips on her neck, chest, ears, and lips.

Dark clouds formed in the distance. Over chains clanging, children yelling, and the raucous calls of the animals, Sarah thought she heard thunder. The land needed rain. The further west they traveled the more the badly needed grass turned brown and bristly. The water in the wagons was perilously low.

And to make her mood even worse, he hadn't done more than ride past in the morning, tipping his hat in his usual dapper way. Only once did he check on her wheels, and then it was when she was with Greta.

What was wrong with him? Was he truly sorry he'd kissed her? If he was trying to convince her the evening had meant nothing to him, then he was fooling himself. The evidence of his arousal was still imprinted against her stomach. No man in such condition could say he wasn't affected.

Had he gone back to 'just being friends'? If it were the case, at least friends talked to each other. She could just smack the man—if he ever got close enough. The way she missed his kisses, she'd probably yank his head down and plant a good one on his mouth—and it didn't matter who watched.

Sarah licked her dry lips. Who on earth would want to kiss lips so cracked they bled, or lips covered in axle grease to keep them from splitting? With the wind blowing dust around, her lips were coated with grease *and* covered in dust.

The only one interested was the one she wished would stay away. After the night of the dance, Horace was more persistent in his pursuit. His comments about kissing bordered on insulting. Had he seen her and Jack? At least Horace hadn't touched her—yet. The way he curled his fingers into his palms when he talked to her as if he were itching to lay a hand on her, made her want to cover herself from head to foot in several layers of clothing. Maybe dress as a man.

Then there was Horace's attitude toward Tommy, as if her son were coming between them. She'd been keeping Tommy in the wagon and out of the sun and dust and away from Horace as much as she could. She was sick of walking, sick of her blasted oxen, and sick of the dust coating everything inside and out. As soon as they hit water, everyone would be soaking their dried-out wagon wheels, as well as their cracked skin.

The dark clouds, almost purple in color, loomed closer. A bolt of lightning streaked across the sky, followed by a roll of thunder. The storm was getting closer. With the sun still shining in the east and the storm approaching from the west, an eerie feeling settled in her chest.

Something was wrong. The wind stopped, but clouds whipped overhead, obscuring the sun. The wagons in front of her halted.

"Whoa, Rose. Whoa Tulip." She pulled on the harness. A man galloped through the wagons.

"Unhitch, unhitch. A cyclone is a-comin'. Circle the wagons. A cyclone is a-comin'." With his arms flapping, man and horse raced away.

"Mommy, what's wrong?" Tommy peeked his head between the opening in the canvas.

"Stay inside, Tommy. A bad storm is coming." Barely glancing at the rapidly darkening sky, she tried unhitching the oxen's yoke. With their eyes rolled back in their heads, both Rose and Tulip fought her. "Damn it. Not now!"

The earth shook beneath her feet. Were bison trying to outrun the storm? As quickly as the wind stopped, it roared to life. Dust and dried grass slammed into her. The oxen jerked from her hands, threatening to run off. Should she get Tommy out of the wagon and let the oxen have their heads?

At a loss of what to do, she nearly gave up, when a pair of muscular arms grabbed the yoke, opened it, and slapped the oxen on their hind quarters.

"Get Tommy," Jack yelled above the pandemonium. "Get beneath the wagon and cover your heads."

As he yanked the wagon into place in the circle, she grabbed Tommy. The noise was so loud, she barely heard his cries. "It's okay. We'll be safe."

She prayed they would be. Nearly tossing her son underneath the wagon, she followed and lay over him, pulling her skirt over their heads. The wagon shook. Pots hanging on the side rattled and clanged. An arm came around her.

"We're going to be all right," he yelled in her ear. "Keep your head down. Even though the cyclone is passing to the west of us, we're still going to be hit by high winds."

Having Jack talking to her and practically laying on top of her and Tommy, gave her a sense of security. Even as the wind buffeted them, sending loose items rolling across the ground, she knew they'd be safe with him there.

The storm screamed and bellowed around them, making further conversation impossible. Dirt assaulted her side when, for an interminable second, the wagon rose then dropped back down. Jack jerked and grunted.

Beneath her Tommy shook. She kissed the side of his head, the only thing she could do to assure him.

It seemed as if hours passed before the wind slowed. Jack never let go of her the entire time. Thank goodness it was dark enough to hide the fact that her bloomers were showing.

She flipped back her skirt from her head and chanced a peek from beneath the wagon. Drops of rain hit the parched earth, sending up puffs of dust. First one, then two, then a deluge.

Jack slid away from her, then came back. "There's no thunder or lightning, and the rain is coming straight down. We need to take advantage of the rain and open the rain barrels."

Sarah scooted backward. The rain drenched her legs, then her back the instant she was exposed, washing away the dust and dirt. The cold water was delightful, refreshing, and the best thing she'd felt since they'd left the river a week ago.

She removed the rain barrel lid, turning up her face and letting the water stream over her skin. She flipped the soaked brim of her bonnet from her forehead. Mud splashed over Tommy's clothes as he jumped up and down. So much for the rain cleaning them.

With the lid leaning against a wheel, she took in the damage. A rip in her canvas could be easily sewn closed. A kettle was missing, but then she wasn't cooking, anyway. She'd have to remove the items from the inside where the rain was pouring in. Other than that, they'd fared the storm well.

Or so she thought until Jack limped to her side. "What happened? Are you all right?"

He held his leg up and rolled his ankle back and forth. "Damn wheel hit me when it came back down."

Guilt washed through her. If he hadn't come to their aid, he wouldn't have been injured. "Take your boot off and let me look at it."

Water swirled around the brim of his hat and down his back. He glanced around them. "I'll be fine. There are others in worse shape than me."

As quickly as the storm had attacked, it stopped, the wall of rain moving east across the prairie.

"Are you guys all right?" Greta asked, trudging through the mud with her family. "I've never been so scared in my entire life." She looked over Sarah's shoulder and gasped.

Sara followed Greta's line of sight. "Oh, no!"

Half the wagons had been tossed on their sides, their wheels spinning. Bags of flour spilled from ripped canvases. Drops of water pinged on kettles and dishes were flung about the area. Splintered rain barrels, smashed canvas bows, and yokes were scattered among other debris.

"Folks," Mr. Hunt called out, "we're going to spend a few days here to assess the damage and make repairs. It's still a week before we arrive at Fort Laramie, so the sooner we can head out the better. Everyone round up their cattle, and we'll start making repairs. My men will help wherever they can."

People scattered to gather their belongings. Children were sent in pairs to collect items strewn by the storm. Sarah picked up one of Tommy's shirts from the ground and rung out the water, snapped it in the air, and draped it over a wheel. She paused. Someone stood behind her. Prickles rose on the back of her neck when a hand clamped on her shoulder.

"Hey, Miz Sarah."

Dammit. *Horace.* She shrugged his hand away. "What do you want, Mr. Manny?"

"Just checkin' on you to make sure you're all right. I can help you if'n you want."

Keeping her back to the man, she noticed Jack talking with Sam. Why wouldn't he turn around and see Horace was pestering her again? Since Jack hadn't bothered to show up for a week, he wouldn't know the man was being more of a nuisance.

"I'm fine. Tommy's fine. My wagon is fine. Why don't you go help the others?" Or go jump off the nearest cliff—if there had actually been one on the flat prairie.

Horace ran a finger down her forearm. "'Cause I'd rather be helping you."

Did she dare elbow him in the stomach? Stomp on his foot? Slam the back of her head into his face and break his nose?

"Mommy, Mommy." Tommy ran up to her. His freckles stood out against his pale face.

Thank heavens for little interrupters. "What honey?" She knelt in front of him.

"Go away, kid. Your mother and I are talking."

Sarah glared at Horace over her shoulder. What did he have against her son? "Mr. Manny, you will not talk to my son like that."

"He's mean like Daddy," Tommy said, his bottom lip trembling.

Horace clamped his hand on Tommy's shoulder and jerked him away from her.

"Why you little brat." He pulled his hand back to hit him. "I'll teach you to talk about your elders like that."

Sarah jumped to her feet and dug her fingers into the back of Horace's hand. "Mr. Manny! You unhand my son right this second before I do something you'll regret."

Horace's chuckle was weak. The anger in his eyes wasn't. He moved his hand and rubbed the back of his neck. "Lady, there isn't anything you can do to me I'd regret." His eyes raked her from head to toe.

If only she could hit him. Knock him into the mud and get in a few well-placed kicks. But she didn't want Tommy to learn to solve problems with violence. Besides, the man was bigger than her and would probably hit her back. "What is your problem with my son, Mr. Manny?"

"I hate kids. They just get in the way of more," he licked his lips and leered at her, "pleasant activities. You know like . . ."

"Mr. Manny! This is neither the time nor the place for this discussion. Now go do something productive like helping right the wagons."

Horace tipped his soggy hat. "You name the time and place, little lady, and I'll be there." With a sneer at Tommy, he headed toward the overturned wagons.

Sarah couldn't repress a shudder. Now she had to fear for herself and worry about Tommy. Horace was like those lions she'd read about who killed the father, then the babies of a lioness so he could breed his own. Bile rose in her throat. There was no way she would let him harm her son.

"Is everything all right, Sarah?" Jack nodded toward Horace's retreating back. "Is he bothering you again?"

Irritation swept through her. What did he care? If he was so worried about Horace, why hadn't he stopped each day to check on her? "He just wanted to make sure we weren't hurt."

If she told him about the conversation, he'd probably beat up Horace. Then again, maybe not. Their shared kiss last week must not have meant as much to him as her. But he had shown up when the storm hit to protect them. Oh, fiddlesticks. She was so confused.

"Sarah." He took off his hat. "I'm sorry I haven't been stopping by each day. I . . ."

"Hey, Billabard," Sam called. "We need you to help with the wagons."

"Be right there," he called over, then met her gaze. "I'd like to talk with you afterward if that's okay. I'll help you clean up."

Sarah took in her surroundings. Her wagon had survived quite well considering the attack by the storm. "I don't really need any help. Tommy and I will give a hand to the others who need it more. If you want to stop later, we can talk after Tommy is asleep."

Jack slapped on his hat. "Later, then."

Chapter Ten

The sun dipped lower in the sky, the red, orange, and pink swirls colliding together to make a breathtaking view. Sarah leaned against the wagon wheel arms crossed over her chest. The wagon master had come around informing everyone that they would be leaving tomorrow as usual. With everyone pitching in and working hard, wagons had been fixed, and what belongings were found scattered about the prairie returned to their rightful owners.

Sarah clutched her shawl over her chest. Even with the heat of the day radiating from the ground, cold seeped into her bones. Between wondering what Jack wanted to talk to her about, worrying about what Horace might do to her and Tommy, and the storm, her nerves were shot. She refused to think about having to marry Mr. Sampson, since it was still months away.

Would Jack kiss her again tonight? Tingles spread from her scalp to her toes, settling in the place between her legs. Lordy, could he kiss. Maybe they could do more than kiss.

The idea of him touching her breasts, skimming his hands over her skin, made her heart skip a beat. Her stomach quivered thinking about touching him. Would his muscles be hard and muscular, not soft and squishing like Peter's? Did he have a hairy chest? Her nipples hardened at the thought of rubbing her breasts against him.

The sun dipped lower, now nearly at the horizon. The camp was settling down. Fires were extinguished. Wagons creaked as people retired for the night. Mothers made last calls to children. Even the animals settled down. Daisy's soft snoring came through the wagon.

She was definitely going to have puppies, and soon, if her fat belly was any indication. Hopefully, she'd wait until they reached Fort Laramie, where the train would rest for a few days.

"How are you tonight, Sarah?"

She jumped and slammed her hand over her heart. "Jack! Oh, my, you scared me."

"Sorry. I guess the mud deadened the sound of my footsteps." He stood beside her and stared at the sunset. "Rough day."

"You could say that."

"Sorry I wasn't more of a help to you and Tommy."

She huffed a breath. "You don't need to be sorry. You were busy helping with the wagons and rounding up animals. You did what you had to do; I did what I had to."

How she wanted to touch him, but a woman didn't make the first move. "I certainly didn't and don't expect you to take care of me. Besides, you were there to help protect us from the storm."

Jack stayed silent. What was he thinking?

"How's your leg?" she asked.

"A little sore. It's nothing more than a bruise." He shrugged. "I'll live. Can we go for a walk? I need to talk to you."

Sarah pushed away from the wheel and followed him to a small group of trees far enough away to not be overheard, yet close enough so she was able to keep an eye on her wagon and Tommy. She didn't trust Horace to try something, and if her son woke up, she could get to him quickly.

With his back to her, Jack tossed his hat to the ground and raked his fingers through his hair. He faced her. "Sarah, I need to explain a few things."

"All right, I'm listening." She leaned against a tree as he paced before her.

"I'm attracted to you."

Her heart skipped a beat.

"I'm not sure why, but I am."

Well, maybe it wasn't quite the way to endear a woman to a man. "Maybe it's because I'm beautiful, witty, charming, and can cook over a campfire with the best of them?"

He stopped and chuckled. "At least the first three are right."

Warmth spread through her. A woman could never be told enough that she was beautiful.

"I was married once." He continued his pacing. "Lily and my parents were best friends. We grew up together. Falling in love with her was as natural as breathing. Our life together was going to be an adventure." He paused and ran a hand down the back of his neck.

"We bought some land north of Fort Laramie, built a cabin and barn, and began to ranch. Life was good. Then she got pregnant."

Sarah didn't know what to say because she knew what had happened to his wife. She didn't want him to know Greta had talked about him, so she kept silent.

"I was so damned excited. I was going to be a father. Toward the end of her pregnancy, I took her to Fort Laramie where there would be other women and a doctor to help her." His laugh was dark. "There was no way in hell I wanted to deliver a baby. I was a rancher, not a doctor."

Sarah recalled how Peter had left the cabin during her labor time. "I suppose delivering a baby *would* be slightly different than delivering a calf or colt."

As if he hadn't heard her attempt at levity, Jack went on. "A month before she was due, we headed into Fort Laramie. There is barely a road from my place, just a path. With her in the back, I went slow so as not to jar her and the baby. Instead of a day's ride, we took nearly three. Halfway there a storm hit. Even though it was summer, the rain was cold, the wind sliced through us. We stopped and burrowed beneath our slickers.

"The next day Lily started sniffling, then coughing. By the time we got to the fort, she was feverish and coughing so hard, she could barely walk." He tipped his head back and stared at the star-filled sky. Tears ran down the side of his cheek, onto his neck, and disappeared into the collar of his shirt. "I took her straight to the doctor's office. Her cold turned into pneumonia, and she went into labor. For two days she fought to bring our son into the world."

A sob caught in the back of Sarah's throat. Except for Tommy, she couldn't imagine loving another person as much as he loved his wife or having someone love her that way.

"Even though the doctor and women in the room insisted I leave, I couldn't. I wanted to be there to see our child being born. I wanted to be with her to help her through the pain." He stared at his hand and flexed his fingers. "She gripped my hand so hard, I had bruises. I didn't know she was so strong. Through her pain she told me how much she loved me; how much she was looking forward to being a mother to our child.

"Except for when she was pushing, she stared into my eyes, as if she wanted to pass her love into me. She stared into them as our son was born. The last thing I told her was there would never be anyone else like her."

Jack's voice dropped to a whisper. "Stared into them as the blood drained from her body, and she no longer had the strength to keep them open. Until she no longer had life." He sunk to his knees and dipped his head until his chin hit his chest. "There was so much blood. I'll never forget the smell. Someone had wrapped the baby in a blanket and put him in Lily's arms. I couldn't understand why they would do that when Lily was gone until I realized the baby wasn't breathing.

"It took the doctor and three other men to pull me away from the room. I vaguely remember striking out at anyone in my way. I only wanted to crawl into that bed with my wife and son."

Sarah had never seen a man cry before and his sobs filled her with pain. Tears pooled in her eyes as she knelt on the ground next to him. "I'm so sorry you lost them." She smoothed her hand up and down his trembling back like she did when Tommy fell and needed comforting. Jack seemed to accept the comfort. Would he accept a hug?

"So now do you understand, Sarah." His words came out in a shudder.

"Understand what?"

"Why I can't be with you."

What was he talking about? Did he mean he still loved his wife so much; he could never be with another woman? Or was it he didn't think she could understand losing a spouse. He would be right. It sounded as if his marriage was nothing like hers, so her being relieved Peter had died couldn't compare to his losing someone he loved with all his heart. It would probably be best to be honest with him.

"I'm not sure I understand."

He shrugged her hand away from his shoulder. "I can't put another woman through that."

"Through what?"

Jack jumped to his feet. "Don't you get it? It was my fault she died."

Viewing him from her perch on the ground, he seemed much taller, commanding, his scowl a bit frightening. "I'm not sure how you believe her death was your fault."

Jack kicked at a rock. "I'm the one who got her with child. I'm the one who decided to take her to Fort Laramie early. If I hadn't she wouldn't have gotten sick and had the baby early. She and our son would still be here."

Sarah's long skirts tangled around her legs as she tried to stand. Jack paced before her as if she weren't there, ignoring her outstretched hand. "Could you please help me up?"

After sitting on the ground for a few seconds, she hiked up her skirts, rolled to her knees, struggled to her feet, and placed a hand on his arm. "Jack. Listen to me."

With blank eyes, he stopped. His lack of reaction scared her. She slapped him on his chest and took a step back when his eyes finally refocused.

"You can't blame yourself for their deaths."

"Why not? They'd still be here if it weren't for me."

"Did you love Lily?"

He hung his head. "Yes, with all my heart."

"Did she love you?"

"I know she did."

How did she explain? Men and women didn't discuss the bedroom side of marriage, especially virtual strangers. Somehow she needed to get through to him. "When two people love each other, one of the results of their love is a child. You did nothing more than share your love through having a child."

Jack shook his head then glanced at her. "Maybe."

"When you decided to take Lily to Fort Laramie early, didn't you do it because you loved her and were worried about her?"

He huffed a breath. "That and the fact that I was scared to deliver the baby myself."

"Scared you couldn't do it or scared because you loved her?"

"Both."

"When you decided to go to Fort Laramie, did you know there was going to be a storm?"

"Hell, no. How could I possibly know?" He turned his back on her.

Sarah's heart leapt in her throat. Good. Maybe he'll understand what she was going to say. "So, if you didn't know there was going to be a storm, how can you possibly be responsible for her getting sick from being caught in one? Many women die in childbirth. From all the blood you said there was, she might have died if you'd stayed at your cabin. Then you'd be blaming yourself for *not* taking her to the fort. Either way, you're taking responsibility for something you had no control over."

He glanced over his shoulder at her. "You don't understand the guilt I feel."

"I do understand the guilt, only mine is different."

He pivoted to face her, creases forming in his forehead. "What would you have to feel guilty about?"

Sarah sighed and this time she turned her back on him. She plucked a leaf from a tree and stripped it from the stem piece-by-piece. "You may have guessed from things Tommy said that my marriage wasn't a good one. Peter spent most of his nights drinking and being with loose women. He didn't like me or Tommy.

"We had a big fight the night he died. He wanted to take Tommy to the tavern to sing for money. I protected my son. After Peter left I wished he'd never return. Can you imagine the guilt I felt when he didn't? I didn't wish him dead, only gone."

Jack stood behind her and put his hands on her shoulders. "How did he die?"

"He was drunk as usual. He and a bunch of men bet on who could race down Main Street the fastest. It had been snowing. The streets were slippery. The horse fell. Peter was thrown. He broke his neck."

Shivers ran down her spine when he spoke into her ear.

"Did you tell him to get on a horse while drunk and ride down a slippery street all hell bent for leather?"

She shook her head.

"Did you wish for him to die?"

"No, but . . ."

Jack spun her around to face him and kneaded her shoulders. "So why should you feel guilty? You didn't do anything wrong."

Sarah poked him in the chest. "My point exactly. Why should you feel guilty for Lily's death when everything you did was because you loved her? Sometimes guilt is simply a way of handling events in our life that are out of our control."

After a moment of silence while he searched her face, his lips turned up at the corners. He nodded. "You're right. I didn't do anything wrong." He released her and took a step back. "Except I made a promise to myself. I would never fall in love again or get a woman with child to have her die."

Sarah rubbed her forehead. "What does that have to do with me?"

"I'm attracted to you. I don't want to hurt you, so I've decided once we get to Fort Laramie, I'm leaving the wagon train and going back to my place." He kept his head down.

Sarah's heart sank like a distant falling star crashing to Earth. She was attracted to him, too, and it shouldn't matter if he was leaving the train. She didn't love him and was getting married in a few months. So, why did it hurt so much?

It would probably be better to let him go. What if her future husband didn't excite her the way Jack did? What if this was her only chance to find out what it was like being made love to? Maybe she was being a hussy, but she wanted to be sure his kisses weren't a fluke.

"Jack?"

After a moment's pause, he glanced up. "What?"

"I have a request."

A corner of his lips quirked up. "I think I'm afraid to ask."

Sarah stood in front of him and placed her palm on his chest. "Would you kiss me again?"

Jack raked his fingers through his hair. "Why?"

"Because I want something to remember you by."

"Aren't you going to be married in a few months?"

"To a man I don't know. It's not as if I'm going to him as a virgin." She clutched his shirt in her fist. "Please. Just one kiss."

When Sarah thought he'd turn away, he grasped her shoulders and pulled her against him.

"Aww, hell," he murmured before he covered her lips with his.

His kiss was as hot, demanding, and as drugging as she remembered. A shudder passed through her. Even if Mr. Sampson were the best lover in the world, she'd never forget Jack's kisses. He swept his tongue over her lips and urged her to open her mouth. She let him in. Sparks radiated through her system, settling in her lower regions. Lights sparkled behind her eyelids, like candles flickering in a breeze. Wait. Lights?

A FLICKER OF LIGHTS brought Jack out of the sexual haze enveloping him. His limbs were weak. His cock ready to explode. As much as he wanted to lay her down, bury himself inside her, and relieve the throbbing in his groin, he couldn't. He'd made a promise to his wife. He broke the kiss.

"Jack," she whispered, tugging on his shirt. "Look."

Had someone seen them kissing? Was Manny lurking behind a tree watching them, ready to pounce?

"Open your eyes. It's amazing."

Doing as she asked, he said, "The tree? You see it, too?" As if unable to believe his eyes, Jack shook his head. "I always thought it was a dream."

Sarah nodded, and holding his hand, touched one of the shimmering leaves. Long branches cloaked them in a secure cocoon, where nothing mattered but the two of them. Warmth spread from her hand, up his arm, settling in his heart. His breath caught.

"Did you feel that?" Sarah's eyes shimmered. "The tree is telling us something."

Jack wasn't sure what the tree was telling her. To him, the tree whispered, "love her." Or maybe it was his imagination; since he wanted to do nothing more than make love with Sarah. The many reasons why he shouldn't touch her melted away.

He cupped her face. "Yes," he whispered before drawing her into another kiss. The world beyond the branches ceased to exist. It was just him, Sarah, and a wagonload of lust.

Sarah broke the kiss. "I want you." She unbuttoned his shirt's top button. "Here." Second button. "Now."

His cock surged with each button she released, until his chest was bared to her roaming hands and he was ready to explode. He hadn't been touched by a woman since his wife died. He would probably respond to any woman like this, so it couldn't be Sarah.

The tree hummed. Had he actually heard it call him a liar? Impossible. Trees didn't talk, but something was surely happening within its shelter.

He smoothed his hands down Sarah's shoulders and cupped her breasts. Through the fabric, her nipples pebbled. Even though he was as hard as he'd ever been, his cock strained even harder against his trousers.

SARAH'S BREATH HITCHED. Could he feel her heart pounding against her rib cage? The way her body reacted to him was new and exciting. Was this what she'd been missing all these years? She wanted him on top of her, inside her. "My legs won't hold me. I need to lie down."

"Then by all means, let's lie down."

They faced each other on the quilt, chest to chest, hip to hip. Tingles zapped from her nipples to her toes and every place in between as he ravaged her with his tongue.

Jack's fingers fumbled with the small buttons of her blouse until she finally pushed his hands away and finished the job for him. In seconds he slid the top down her shoulder, taking the strap of her chemise along with it. Warm air caressed her exposed breast.

His kiss deepened as he cupped her breast, molding it into his large hand. He tweaked her nipple, sending shards of desire spiraling through her.

Sarah moaned when he moved his mouth from her lips to her breast, licking then sucking her nipple. Her other breast ached for the same attention.

"Delicious," he said, inching his hand down her leg, raising her skirt higher and higher until it was at her waist. He slipped his hand into her bloomers, moving lower and lower until his fingers reached her most private parts.

Jack pressed her onto her back. "Spread your legs, Sarah."

As if she had a choice since her legs separated without any thought on her part. He toyed with her hair, then skimmed a finger between her folds.

Sensations like she'd never experienced before shot through her body. Her skin was on fire. Her nerve endings boiled. Her heart was surely going to explode from her chest. Would she ever be able to catch her breath?

He slid in one finger, then another. Her body shattered. She bit her bottom lip to keep from screaming out as wave after wave of intense pleasure rocked her world.

JACK EASED SARAH'S bloomers down her legs and tossed them to the side. He was ready to erupt. His cock was so hard, it hurt. Watching and listening to Sarah coming was as exciting as coming himself. While Lily said she enjoyed their lovemaking, she'd never let loose like Sarah.

He unbuttoned his pants and slid them down to his knees. Finesse was not in order tonight. "I'm not sure I can wait any longer."

He pressed the tip of his cock at her opening and hesitated. What if he got her pregnant? Then Sarah bucked her hips and gripped his ass. He was lost. With one quick shove, he was buried to the hilt. His mind centered on nothing but the pulsing of her muscles around his cock. Only Sarah and her heat.

Pleasure overrode the pain of her nails digging into his ass. His balls tightened. His entire body shuddered, and with a shameless groan, he spilled inside her.

For a few moments nothing filled the air except their ragged breaths.

"That was amazing," Sarah finally said, her voice soft and sultry.

Jack rolled from her and settled next to her, dropping his arm over his eyes. Amazing didn't come close to what he'd experienced. He couldn't come up with any other words to describe the most intense orgasm of his life.

"Jack?"

"Hmmm?" His brain still wasn't functioning properly. He wasn't sure who this guy was she asked for but figured he'd better answer.

"The tree is gone."

Moving his arm from his eyes was near to impossible, yet he managed to drag it away. Sure enough, the tree was gone. How the hell could it appear and disappear? Were they crazy? And when had Sarah seen the tree before?

Sarah leaned up on her elbows. "Do you smell that?"

A warm breeze brought the scent of smoke to him. "Someone has a fire."

She glanced over him at the circle of wagons. "At this time of the night?"

"Jack," she whispered. "Look."

Jack rolled over and stared into the night lit by a full moon. A person skulked around Sarah's wagon.

"Yeah, I see him." He recognized the man's ragged hat. Horace. Shit, what was he doing? A red light flickered briefly. Flames. He was going to kill Manny if it was the last thing he did.

Sarah jerked on her bloomers and searched for her blouse. "Oh, my God. Tommy."

He yanked up his pants, buttoning them as he charged toward her wagon. He couldn't let another person he cared for die. Behind him Sarah screamed for her son.

"Get Tommy," he yelled, tearing around the side. The wagon dipped when Sarah climbed up the front. He ripped the cover from the water barrel, grabbed a bucket, and filled it. It took only one bucket to put out the small fire on the ground at the end of the wagon. He stomped on the wet embers to make sure no errant, hot ashes restarted.

By the time Sarah came to him, holding Tommy to her chest, people were climbing from their beds to see what the ruckus was all about. Jack turned his back, buttoned his shirt, and jammed it into his pants.

Sarah must have tidied up in the wagon, as her blouse was fastened properly and tucked into her skirt.

"Is Tommy all right?" Greta stood beside Sarah holding a shawl tightly at her neck.

"Mommy, my eyes hurt."

Sarah rubbed Tommy's back as she had done to him a bit ago. Her gentle touch was still etched in his skin.

"Shhh, sweetie. You'll be fine. They'll stop hurting soon."

"What happened?" Greta asked.

"Get out of my way. What's going on here?" Horace shoved through the crowd and pushed Jack out of the way. "Sarah, honey. Are you all right? I came as soon as I heard about the fire." He rounded on Jack. "What the hell did you do this time, Billabard?"

Was Manny serious? Was he actually going to put the blame for the fire on him? Jack folded his arms over his chest. Instead of answering, he'd wait him out to see what lies the jackass would come up with.

"Sarah, honey," Horace reached for Sarah's son, "let me take Tommy from you. He must be getting heavy."

Jack bit back a laugh at Horace's syrupy words. Sarah narrowed her eyes and held Tommy away from him.

"I've told you before, Mr. Manny, and I'll tell you again in front of all these people. I never gave you permission to call me Sarah. I'm not your honey, sweetheart, little woman, or any other endearment you call me."

Horace slapped a hand to his chest as if Sarah had injured him. Jack put a hand over his mouth. Horace was quite the actor. And Sarah was gorgeous when angry. He'd let her have her say then step in if Manny so much as looked at her wrong.

"But honey . . . I mean Mrs. Nickelson," he quickly added when Sarah tightened her lips. "This man started a fire by your wagon. Why you and Tommy might have been killed. I would simply die if something happened to either of you." Horace pointed a finger at Jack. "Why first he loosens your wheel, then tries to burn down your wagon. You can't trust him. Come with me, and I'll take care of you."

Someone's cough sounded more like a laugh. Jack searched the crowd and settled on Greta's husband, who rolled his eyes at him.

"Here." Sarah passed Tommy to Greta and took a step toward Horace, who smiled as if he was going get what he wanted. "Mr. Billabard did not loosen my tire, nor did he set this fire."

Horace puffed out his chest and hitched up his pants. "Is that what *he* told you, because I have evidence he did. He'll say anything to get you to spread your legs for him."

Gasps and mumbling came from several onlookers. Jack took a step forward, ready to grab the man by the collar. Sarah shook her head at him, and he stopped. Narrowing his eyes, he fought down his anger. He'd let her handle it . . . for now.

Sarah took another step toward Horace, who backed up. Jack relaxed, and this time he bit back a chuckle. It must be finally sinking into Manny's dull brain how angry she was.

"Let me ask you something, Mr. Manny." Sarah tapped a finger to her lips. "Were you on duty tonight?"

"Well, yes, I was."

"And where were you stationed?"

"West of here, about a quarter mile from the train."

Sarah paced before him. "Hmmm. My wagon is one of the furthest from there. Right?"

Horace nodded then frowned as if he had no idea where this was going. Jack did, and he was enjoying every second of Sarah's interrogation.

"So can you tell me how you found out about the fire and got here so quickly?" Sarah looked around at the crowd. "I mean some of these good people barely got out of their beds before you arrived. Were you really patrolling?"

Jack took a step forward when, without answering her question, Horace pivoted to Jack and jerked his finger at him. "You. You're the one who is causing all the problems here, Billabard. If it weren't for you, Sarah would be mine."

Jack didn't have time to grab Sarah before she attacked Manny.

"Why you little jackass. I never was, nor will I ever be yours." She shoved him against her wagon. "I've told you over and over to leave me alone. Mr. Billabard has nothing to do with this. You're the one who loosened my wheel and you're the one who set the fire. You're the one who wants my son out of the way so you can have me." Sarah poked him in the chest. "You." Poke. "Will." Poke. "Never." Poke. "Have." Poke. "Me."

Jack smiled. At the rate she was going, Manny was going to have a mass of bruises on his chest. He didn't care one way or the other about Manny. He did need to stop her before her finger fell off from touching the asshole.

Jack tugged her away. "That's enough, Sarah."

Horace held his clenched fists at his sides then before anyone could do anything, grabbed Sarah's hair. "You bitch!"

Anger nearly blinded Jack. He grabbed Manny's hand holding Sarah and squeezed his wrist until he let go of her, then tossed Manny to the ground. "Don't you ever touch Mrs. Nickelson or anyone else on this train again."

Horace jumped to his feet, fists swinging.

"What is going on here?" Sam yelled, rushing through the group. "Manny, why aren't you patrolling?"

"Because," Horace pointed a finger at Jack, "he started a fire by Mrs. Nickelson's wagon, and I'm making sure he pays for his crime. He also loosened her wheel a few weeks back."

Sam faced Jack. "Is this true?"

"You know me better than that, Sam. I would never do anything to harm anyone, especially a widowed woman and her son."

"Horace?" Sam raised his eyebrows.

"He's lying."

Sarah stepped between the two men. "Jack didn't do those things. I'm not positive who loosened the tire, but I know for sure Mr. Manny set the fire."

Sam restrained Horace from going after Sarah. "I did not. Billabard did."

"Mr. Hunt, I recognized Mr. Manny moving around my wagon. Shortly after I smelled smoke."

"How could you tell it was me?" Horace said between tight lips. "You was in the wagon."

"No, I wasn't. I was over by the trees. I recognized your decrepit hat. No one here wears a hat as disgusting as yours."

Horace laughed. "It's a widder woman's word against mine, and you know how they are."

Jack crossed his arms over his chest but stood ready to punch Manny if he attacked Sarah again. "No, we don't, Manny. Why don't you tell everyone here how widows are."

"Why they ask for it." Horace took in the people observing the interaction. He hitched up his pants. "If'n you know what I mean."

Jack shook his head. "I guess I don't rightly know what you mean, Manny. Why don't you explain it for us."

"Well, see'n as how they don't have a man to take care of their needs, they look for someone, anyone, to satisfy 'em. The longer they go without a man, the more desperate they become. Mrs. Nickelson here has been beggin' for it." Horace pointed to his chest. "And I'm just the man to give her what she wants."

Sarah leapt at Horace and slapped him across the cheek. "Why you vile snake. I wouldn't go with you if you were the last man on Earth. You're dirty, stinky, and disgusting. I have never sought you out and told you time and time again I'm not interested. Why can't you understand that?"

Horace rubbed his face. "You'll be sorry you did that, missy. No woman slaps me and gets away with it."

Greta stepped forward. "What Sarah says is true. I've heard the comments he's made to her. Comments that no gentleman would make to a lady, and Sarah is a lady, through and through. Many times I've told him myself to leave her alone. He never listened and always came slinking back like the snake he is."

Jack had enough of Manny's lies. "I also saw him at Sarah's wagon tonight just before we noticed smoke coming from the back."

"See." Horace jumped up and down, pointing between Jack and Sarah. "I told you she was a hussy. She was with Billabard."

A few murmurs rose from the crowd.

While lying was not one of Jack's best suits, now was the time to do the best he could to protect Sarah. Heat crept up his neck and face.

Hopefully, it wouldn't be noticeable by the nosy onlookers in the full moon.

"Yes, Sarah and were together, talking. Since I'm leaving the train when we reach the fort, she wanted to know what to expect for the rest of the trip."

When no one said anything, he took it as a sign they believed him. He didn't dare look at Sarah, but her quick breath said volumes. Would he see anger at his announcement of his leaving? Did she think their time together would change things? "Manny didn't know we had a good view of the camp, or Tommy could have died from the smoke. I'm not sure what his purpose was, but he is the one who set the fire. I also know he loosened her wheel. I recognized his boots that night."

"Why would you have seen his boots?" Sam asked.

Jack put his hands in his pockets and stared at Manny. "I knew what he was saying about her and worried what he might do, so I'd been bedding down outside her wagon to make sure he didn't go after her in the dark."

Sarah gasped. "I didn't know you did that."

"We've been keeping an eye on her, too," Greta added.

The edge of something pink and frilly, looking like the leg of a woman's undergarment, draped from the corner of Horace's pocket. What kind of man walked around with a woman's garment in his pocket?

"What's that in your pocket, Manny?" Jack nodded at Horace's pants.

Horace put his hand over the object and sneered. "That's none of your damn business."

Jack frowned. "Didn't look like anything to me. Looked like something pink and frilly."

Sam scratched his chin and stepped in front of Horace. "Pull it out, Manny." When Horace hesitated, Sam added, "Now."

The women gasped and the men laughed when Horace pulled out a pair of pink bloomers, hooking them over his forefinger.

"Those are mine, you skunk." Anger laced Sarah's words. "How did you get them? From my wagon?"

Horace turned to the crowd and snickered. "Maybe I took them off you, Sarah."

"Why you little . . . I would never let you . . ." Tears slid down her cheeks.

Jack's heart ached at her distress. Comforting her like he wanted would only make things worse for her.

"Where did you get," Sam pointed to the bloomers, "uh, that, uh, thing?"

Horace stuck his stubby nose in the air. "Not tellin."

"It seems to me, Manny, you are in possession of stolen goods. Considering everything else I've heard here tonight, I'm putting you under arrest. Since we're so close to Fort Laramie, we'll have a trial there and decide your fate."

"You bastard!" Horace screamed.

With his hands in his pockets, Jack wasn't prepared for Manny's charge. People stepped back as they crashed to the ground, Manny landing on Jack's chest, pummeling him in the face while Jack tried to take control.

"You son of a bitch. This is all your fault." Horace's spittle spattered Jack's face between the punches. "If it weren't for you, she'd be mine."

Jack arched his back, managing to throw Manny off. With his hands finally free, he pushed himself up from the mud and yanked Manny by the shirt front, hauled him to his feet, and slammed his fist in his face. Manny went down like a felled tree.

Jack's hand hurt, and he'd probably have bruises on his face. But damn, it felt good to finally punch the man out. At least now Manny would be tied up in the lead wagon. Except for necessary breaks, he'd stay confined until they reached Fort Laramie. Knowing Sarah and

Tommy would be safe once the train left the fort would make it easier for him to head home.

"Okay, folks," Sam said, flipping Horace to his stomach and wrapping a rope around his hands, "show is over. Time to head back to your wagons."

At Sam's nod, several men helped him hoist Horace to his feet.

"You haven't seen the last of me, Billabard." Horace spit at Jack's boots, then Sarah's dress. "You neither, woman." His curses dimmed as he was dragged away.

"Are you all right?" Sarah handed Jack his hat and took Tommy from Greta. She'd never understand how he'd slept through the yelling.

Jack brushed mud from the brim. "Except for a few bruises, I'll be fine. I'm sorry you had to see that."

Sarah huffed a breath and put her hand on his arm. "I'm sorry you got hurt protecting Tommy and me." She shifted Tommy higher on her shoulder. "Thank you."

How could the simple warmth of her fingers on his shirt settle in his groin and make him want her again when they'd just been together? Sarah struggled to hold Tommy. Last week he'd have taken the burden from her. Making love with Sarah didn't change the need to move on, only made it harder to do so. His feelings for Sarah didn't change his promise to his wife. "I need to see what damage the fire caused." He turned his back on her and stepped away, ignoring her gasp and struggle to hold Tommy.

"Why don't you let us take Tommy to our wagon," Greta said.

Sarah passed Tommy to Greta's husband. "Night, Mommy. I love you. Night, Mr. Bard. I love you, too."

A piece of Jack's heart melted. He would not, could not tell the boy he loved him back. Seeing as how in a week he'd never see them again, it would be cruel, even though it was true. Instead, he ran his hand over Tommy's back. "Sleep well, young man."

Disregarding Sarah's tear-filled eyes, he peered between the canvas flaps. The inside reeked of smoke. There wouldn't be time to air it out before they left in the morning.

"It doesn't seem too bad." Her voice quivered.

Was she upset about the state of her wagon, or the way he was treating her? She brushed his shoulder with hers as she assessed the damage.

"I can pull back up the sides to let it air out."

There was another problem that would have to be faced. "Where will you sleep tonight?"

Sarah bit her bottom lip. "With Horace locked up, it should be safe enough for me to sleep under the wagon."

Jack tied the canvas back and kicked at the burned-out ashes. "That's true. You know there are those who won't believe we were only talking tonight."

Sarah's blonde hair glittered in the moonlight. His cock flared to life. Even knowing he was leaving, he wanted to take her in his arms. Unbutton those tiny buttons again. Lay her down beneath her wagon and take her slow. Spend more time on her luscious breasts, kiss . . .

"Are you all right?"

Shit. Caught in the act of dreaming of being with Sarah again. Hopefully, she couldn't see his hard-on. He ran a hand down the back of his neck. "I'm fine. Just tired. With the storm and the fire. Well, I'm exhausted." Did he dare bring up their time beneath the tree?

Sarah smoothed a finger over his cheek. "Not to mention the fight with Mr. Manny. You're going to have quite a shiner."

Jack ducked away from her gentle touch. Guilt rushed over him at her quick intake of breath. Shit, now he'd hurt her feelings. Hell, he was sure he'd hurt her earlier when he told everyone he wouldn't be staying with the train. And after the incredible lovemaking with her, leaving was essential for his emotional well-being. He wished he could take off before they reached Fort Laramie. With Manny locked up, it would leave Sam short two men for a week. He couldn't do that to his friend.

In a pretense of checking the wagon's wheels, he put distance between them. He needed to get away from her before he pulled her into his arms and completely lost himself in her. His promise to never love another woman again burned across his mind.

"Jed and some of kids are bunking under their wagon, so you should be safe outside tonight." He slapped on his hat. His head told him he was doing the right thing.

He rubbed his chest. Why did his heart hurt so much?

EVEN THOUGH HE KNEW Sarah and Tommy were safe from Manny, Jack spread out his bedroll nearby. With his hands beneath his head, he watched the constellations move across the sky, keeping his eyes from the woman wrapped in a blanket beneath her wagon.

A small whimper came from inside. Sarah rose and went to the back of the wagon, lifting Daisy to the ground. Without looking around, Sarah lay back down. The dog waddled its over-sized body to do her business. Then with a moan and deep sigh, Daisy curled up at her feet and went back to sleep.

For a few more minutes he imagined himself spooning with Sarah, his cock pressed against her ass. "I give up." Obviously, sleep wasn't going to come tonight. He rose from his bedroll, walked to the trees, and sat with his back against a massive oak. From here he would be able to keep an eye on her.

He was tired, but like the wind blowing down a mountainside, the day's events rolled through his mind. The storm. The fire. Horace. Tommy. Sarah. Always Sarah. Now he could add the exciting way she responded to him, accepted him into her body. Even though he'd never forget it, leaving was the best thing for him to do. She and Tommy had a new future ahead of them in Oregon City, and he couldn't mess it up for them, no matter how he felt about her.

With his decision made, he was able to relax. His shoulders dropped and his hands slipped from his lap as his eyes slid shut.

He jerked, smacking his head against the tree trunk. Damn. He'd fallen asleep. He stood, stretched out his back, and headed for his bedroll. Sleeping on the ground, no matter how hard, was better than bark digging into his back.

Was his bedroll moving? Slowing his step, he peered at his blankets. Sure enough, they were moving. Had a snake found warmth for the night? A prairie dog? Whatever it was, he had no intention of sharing. With the barrel of his rifle, he eased the edge of the blanket back, ready to fight off whatever was hidden.

A small yip greeted him. "Daisy. What . . ." Something small squiggled. Something else squirmed. Daisy whimpered. He pulled back the blanket a little more and stepped back. "Well, I'll be damned."

"What's going on?"

Jack slapped a hand against his chest. How had he not heard Sarah's approach? "Geez, woman. Don't scare me like that."

"Sorry. Why are you standing out here?" Sarah knelt beside his bedroll. "Oh, my. Daisy's having her puppies."

"So, I noticed." He squatted beside her. "In my bedroll, no less."

"Oh, Jack, I'm so sorry." She patted Daisy's side as another puppy eased from her body. "It's all right, girl."

If only his wife had had such an easy time.

"How many has she had so far?" she asked.

"One, two, three . . . Looks like six."

In the silence of the night, he sat beside Sarah, watching in awe as one puppy after another slipped from Daisy's body. He'd seen enough cows, pigs, and horses give birth over the years, yet it never ceased to amaze him. Daisy finally lay still, then lifted her head to clean off her newborns.

"Eleven. Twelve." Sarah shook her head. "How are we ever going to travel with a dozen puppies?"

He laughed. "There's really nothing you have to do, Sarah. Daisy will do all the work."

"Still, that's a lot of dogs."

"By the time you get to Oregon City, they'll be old enough to give away." Would her new husband be willing to take on a boy who is not his own *and* a bunch of dogs? He hoped so.

Sarah fingered one of the pups. "What do we do tonight? We can't leave her out here."

"Do you think she'd let us move her and the puppies to your wagon?"

"I doubt it. New mothers can be extremely protective."

"I guess we could stay and keep an eye on her. I'd hate to see coyotes get her and the pups. " Since he'd just promised himself to stay away from her, it was probably the wrong thing to do, but he couldn't let Sarah sit out her by herself. "Besides, I don't have any place to sleep now."

Sarah rose and headed toward her wagon. "I'll get you a quilt and sit with you."

Jack eyed the sweet sway of her hips as she walked away. "Thanks, Daisy, old girl," he muttered. "How am I supposed to spend the night with Sarah and keep my hands to myself? Couldn't you have had your babies somewhere else?"

Thank heavens Sarah had her quilt and another for him in hand when she came back. At least they would be away from each other and temptation. Well, temptation on his part, anyway.

She wrapped one of the quilts around her shoulders, lay beside Daisy, and petted the dog's side. The puppies rooted for milk. He lowered the brim of his hat to shield his eyes from the scene. Sitting cross legged, he pulled his quilt around himself. As much as he wanted to avoid watching, Sarah's beauty kept his eyes on her.

The full moon shone like a beacon against her hair. A small smile graced her face. It was all too domestic for him. Her hand stilled.

"About tonight, Sarah."

She lifted her head and stared at him. "Yes?"

"I want you to know it was one of the best things that has happened to me in four years."

"Me, too." Her smile warmed his heart.

"It doesn't change anything, though. I need to go back home." He pulled the quilt tighter and stared at the sky. "If there should be a babe from this, make sure you get word to me. You can send a letter to the fort." She was silent for so long, he thought she wasn't going to answer him.

"I'll miss you, Jack."

Had he heard her right? Her words had been nothing more than a whisper. "Did you say something?" She didn't answer. He leaned closer. Her breath was slow and even. She'd fallen asleep. Probably a good thing, because he wanted to kiss those lips and enjoy her body one more time before he left.

Jack lay down on the other side of Daisy. He'd make sure to be up before the camp woke in the morning.

Chapter Twelve

Sarah shaded her eyes against the glaring sun. It had been a week since the storm and fire. Not to mention the incredible night beneath the tree. If her body hadn't been sore the next morning, she'd never believe it had happened. Thankfully, her courses had started. Had she found herself with child she wasn't sure if she wanted to let Jack know. Being married to one man who hadn't wanted her was enough.

Other than a brief tip of his hat as he rode by each morning, she'd seen nothing of Jack. He hadn't even stopped to check on the puppies, much to Tommy's chagrin. Now the adobe walls of Fort Laramie were close. By late afternoon, they would join teepees and a few other wagons whose white covers glimmered in the distance.

Last night, Sam had gathered the men and women and their families to give them an idea of what would happen at the fort.

They would make camp across the Laramie River from the fort. During the day they could go into the post and buy additional supplies, pay for a bath, and post any letters to send home. Everyone, particularly the women, were to stay away from the barracks, especially the bachelor quarters known as Old Bedlam.

Beneath the brim of her bonnet, she'd watched Jack standing on the opposite side of the circle formed for the meeting. She sensed his eyes on her, but his hat shaded his face. Was he regretting his decision to ride away once they reached Fort Laramie or had he changed his mind? Was he anxious to get back to his home and his memories of Lily?

His leaving was probably for the best. Becoming more involved with the man while traveling to marry another was not a wise idea.

Tommy had been subdued most of the week. He cried out at night; afraid another storm was approaching. A wisp of camp smoke made him cling to her. Even though Greta's children tried to get him to play with them, he rarely left her side. The only thing making him happy was Daisy and her puppies. He spent most of his time sitting beside her in the back of the wagon, talking to her and holding the babies.

Now they were hours from the fort and Jack's departure. Every time she thought of it, her heart broke a little more. Tommy had been asking why he didn't stop in the morning anymore. The only explanation she could give was he was too busy working now since Mr. Manny was arrested. Anyway, that was what she kept telling herself.

As the fort loomed closer, a cloud of dust rose as a contingent of soldiers halted by the first wagon. One-by-one the others before her stopped.

Sarah grabbed the yoke. "Whoa, Rose. Whoa, Tulip."

"What are those men doing, Mommy?"

She'd finally enticed Tommy from Daisy's side, and they'd been walking. She took Tommy's hand and moved for a better view. "I don't know, honey." A lone rider came toward them. Wondering why a soldier would ride the line, she was surprised to see Jack dismount. Her heart fluttered as her stomach flipped. Had he changed his mind?

"Mr. Bard! Mr. Bard!" Tommy let go of her hand, raced to Jack, and jumped into his arms, sending him back several steps before they landed in a heap. "I missed you."

Jack leaned up on his elbows and ruffled Tommy's hair. "Missed you, too, cowboy." He lifted Tommy from his stomach and stood.

Tommy picked up his fallen hat. "Why don't you come and see us anymore?"

"I've been busy helping Sam."

"Because Mr. Manny is a bad man?"

Jack chuckled. "Yes." He faced Sarah. "That's what I came to tell you. Sam sent one of the men ahead to the fort to have soldiers come and take Manny to jail. He'll stay there until a judge can come for a trial."

Since he was arrested, Sarah had lived in fear Manny would somehow escape and come after her. Knowing he would be behind bars was a relief. Once they were back on the trail to Oregon City and miles between her and the skunk, she would feel even better. Then an awful thought came to her.

"Will I have to testify?"

Without meeting her eyes, he shook his head. "No. Someone from the fort will write down witness accounts and present them to the judge. There are enough people to testify about his treatment of you and how he attacked me. I'm confident the judge will put him away long enough for you to get settled into your new life." He tipped his hat and headed to his horse.

"Jack, wait."

With one foot in a stirrup, he stopped, keeping his sight on Papaya's back. "What, Sarah?"

"Are you leaving for your home right away?"

"I think it would be for the best."

Tommy tugged on Jack's pants. "You can't go Mr. Bard. I love you."

Sarah's heart broke at the tears running down her son's face. While Sarah didn't love Jack, she definitely liked him a lot. She had a feeling no other man would surpass how he'd made her body sing. The dark circles facing her in her small hand mirror each morning bore testament to a week of sleepless nights.

Jack squatted before Tommy and put his hands on his shoulders. "I'm sorry, cowboy. I have to. I have a ranch to get back to. You'll have a new daddy in Oregon City."

"I don't want to go to 'Gon City. You can take Mommy and me with you." Tommy's bottom lip quivered. "Please, Mr. Bard? I'll be a good boy."

"Oh, Tommy." Jack hugged him, his eyes suspiciously bright. "It has nothing to do with you being a good or bad boy. I don't have room for children at my house. It's too small."

Knowing he and Lily would have lived there after their child was born, Sarah doubted it. It was simply an excuse to run and hide from his feelings.

In the distance the soldiers retreated back to the fort, Horace tied to a horse, his voice ringing out his displeasure. While she couldn't hear exactly what he was yelling, she had a good idea it was about her and Jack.

"That's enough, Tommy." The wheels in the wagon in front of her squeaked as they rolled forward. Sarah tugged on her oxen until they followed. "Mr. Billabard needs to get to work." She gave Jack a pointed look. "*Maybe* he'll stop and say goodbye before he leaves. Won't you, Mr. Billabard?"

Without a word, he tipped his hat, mounted his horse, and galloped away. Sarah bit her bottom lip and swallowed her tears. Would she ever see him again?

THREE DAYS LATER, SARAH walked alongside Tommy, holding his hand, while trying to keep her blasted oxen moving. They'd enjoyed their respite at Fort Laramie too much and had grown lazy. The rest of the trip west was going to be a long one.

"C'mon, you two. Let's get a move on."

"Do we have to go, Mommy?"

"I'm afraid so, honey." With each rotation of her wheels, her heart grew heavier. During their break at the fort, they hadn't seen any sign of Jack. She'd thought maybe he'd show up when they were being questioned about Horace. Searching for him while purchasing supplies to replace those lost in the storm was a lesson in futility. Was he purposely avoiding her? Either Jed or one of his boys accompanied her and Greta to the fort.

She figured he'd at least come to the dance last night to say his goodbyes to, if not for her and Tommy, then the other people he'd met. Despite anticipating his arrival, he hadn't shown. Declining every offer to dance by the single soldiers, she sat on the sidelines with Greta and Tommy.

Besides taking care of essentials while at the fort, she penned a few letters to send back home. Despite their hatred of her, she wrote one to her in-laws, letting them know they'd made it this far. Her letter to Mary Jones was much longer and more detailed.

WITH HER WAGON CLEARED of all smoke and repacked with clean clothes and bedding, the next two days passed slowly. Tommy was distracted and ill-tempered. She understood how he felt. The weather was hot, dry, and dusty. Even with the mountains for a change of scenery, nothing could change the monotony of plodding along. He missed Jack as much as she did. Even the closed-eyed puppies no longer held his interest.

"Sarah," Greta called out, walking alongside the wagon. "Want some company?"

Of course she'd be delighted for her friend's company. Tommy's wiggling and constant questions about Jack were wearing on her already fractured nerves. "Sure. I'd love some. Tommy, why don't you go play with Greta's kids?"

"Don't wanna." He stuck his thumb in his mouth. Since Jack's leaving, he'd gone back to the babyish habit.

"George found a snake he wants to show you."

Tommy's eyes lit up, and he popped out his thumb. "A snake?" In a second he was gone.

"Thanks, Greta. He needed something to get his mind off Jack, and I needed a break from his pouting and bad behavior."

"Tommy's missing him." Greta hooked her arm through Sarah's. With everyone getting ready for the next long leg of the trip, they hadn't had much of a chance to talk since leaving Fort Laramie.

"What about you? I was rather surprised to hear he was leaving the train. I was sure he felt something for you and you for him." Greta waved her hand in front of her face. "If it's going to be hot like this the rest of the trip, I may melt."

How much should she share with Greta without breaking Jack's confidence? He hadn't said not to tell anyone. Besides, Greta was the one who had told her his wife had died. And it wasn't as if she'd ever see the man again. With a teeny bit of guilt Sarah relayed his story from the night nearly two weeks ago, of course leaving out the more personal details.

"So, I'm to understand that he won't give up his promise to never fall in love again after his wife died?"

Sarah nodded.

"Oh, the poor man. I know our marriages were different from his, but he needs to know it's all right to go on with his life, to fall in love again."

Sam walked toward them, stopping briefly at each wagon. Sarah hoped there wasn't more trouble. "I tried to explain to him it wasn't his fault, before we noticed the fire. We didn't have a chance to continue our conversation."

Greta shook her head. "For a man as intelligent as Jack, he sure is stupid." She dug her fingers into Sarah's arm. "And you. You're just as bad."

"Me?" Was Greta kidding? What did she do?

"Yes, you. You could have done more to change his mind. Kiss him more. Give him a little leeway with your body."

"Greta!" On one hand, Sarah was happy her friend obviously hadn't seen them that night. On the other hand, shocked that Greta would suggest such a thing—even if it did happen.

"By now you should know I speak my mind. It was plain as day you two were attracted to each other. If I'd been you and had a sexy man like Jack Billabard interested in me, I would have let him have his wicked way with me. After all, 'you know what widder women are like.'"

Sarah chuckled at Greta's voice sounding like Horace's. "That may be, but this widder woman has a son to think about. Not to mention a man to marry in a few months. What would Mr. Sampson do if I didn't show up? Put his life on hold, waiting for me? It wouldn't be fair."

"Oh pish-posh, Sarah. You could have sent him a letter."

"Did someone say letter?" Sam came to them and matched his stride with theirs. "How did you know I had a letter for you, Sarah?"

"A letter for me?" Who would have sent her a letter way out in the middle of nowhere? Certainly not her in-laws or anyone from home.

"A courier just arrived from out west. He stopped on his way to the fort. I was surprised when I saw this for you." Sam handed over a crumbled, stained paper.

Sarah kept walking as she stared at her name and city scratched in black ink on a piece of paper folded in half. She fingered the wax sealing the two halves together.

Greta nudged Sarah's side. "Open it, for Pete's sake."

Using her thumb and forefinger, Sarah peeled the paper away from the wax and began reading. Heat rushed to her face. Her step faltered. She re-read the simple note.

Mrs. Nickelson, Hope this finds you still in Independence. I have news. I married the woman of my dreams, so you do not need to come to Oregon City. Mr. Frank Sampson

Good heavens, what now? Sarah stopped in her tracks, making Greta re-trace her steps.

"Sarah, what's wrong? You're as white as a sheet."

Should she laugh? Cry? Scream? All of them? She handed the note to Greta and put one foot before the other. One step closer to no future, one step farther away from another.

"Oh, my," Greta said, after a minute. "What are you going to do?"

"I have absolutely no idea." What if she continued on to Oregon City? She had no way of making a living and no man to take care of her. She was in the same predicament if she went back to Independence. Maybe she should head back to Missouri, where at least she knew people. But how? The train was heading west, not east. She certainly couldn't go back by herself.

Greta handed the paper back to Sarah, interrupting her rampant thoughts. "Maybe we should talk to Sam and Jed about this."

If Jack were here. No, she wouldn't think about him. Not now. Not ever. "That sounds like a good idea. Tonight, after supper."

"I'll cook."

As conflicted as she was, Sarah had to laugh. "Good idea. I wouldn't want to make them sick to their stomachs before they came up with a solution to my problem."

THE NEXT DAY AFTER breakfast, Sarah stood before Jed, Greta and their children. "I'm going to miss you all so much." Tommy stood by her side, crying.

Jed pulled her into his arms. "You take care of yourself and Tommy." His sniffle was nearly Sarah's undoing.

After hugging their children, Sarah turned to Greta. "I don't know what I would have done without you, Greta. You . . ." How could she explain how Greta had been like a mother and a friend to her without breaking down and sobbing.

Greta's hug squeezed her ribs to the point of pain. "I know. I know. You've been like a daughter to me, one I didn't have to get through the teenage years." Keeping her hands on Sarah's shoulders, she stepped back. "Now you write and let me know you made it back all right. Find yourself a good man to help you raise Tommy and give you more babies."

A vision of Jack's smiling face passed through her mind. Would she ever find someone kind, funny, and caring like him? Not to mention his kisses and thrilling touches.

"Mrs. Nickelson, it's time to go." Simeon Willis, was taking her back to Fort Laramie.

Last night, it was decided she would go to the fort, and from there, hopefully pick up some emigrants not wanting to venture any further into the wilderness. She may have to wait a while for anyone who couldn't take the rigors of the trail and were heading back east. Sam had written a letter to the post commander explaining her situation and asking him to help her find a safe place to stay while there.

With one last hug to her friends, and a thank you to Sam, Sarah helped Tommy onto the wagon seat and climbed up beside him. She slapped the reins. "C'mon Rose, Tulip. We're heading home, wherever home is."

Chapter Thirteen

Sarah raised her arms and stretched her stiff, aching body toward the bright blue morning sky. She flipped over slices of bacon sizzling in a cast-iron skillet. Rolls, given to her by Greta warmed on the edge of the fire. Coffee bubbled in a blue pot.

Sleep had eluded her all night. Even when the wagon train had settled down for the night, there were always noises. Oxen stomping, cows lowing, and people snoring. Last night there was only a coyote howling in the distance. Mr. Willis, sleeping beneath the wagon with his rifle at his side, hadn't even snored. It was too quiet.

Plus, there was the worry of a lone wagon being attacked, not so much by Indians, but by anyone wanting to steal what she had and maybe even worse.

"Mornin', Mrs. Nickelson."

"Please call me Sarah." She didn't miss his grimace when she handed him a cup of coffee. She grinned at him. "Guess you heard about my cooking skills—or lack of them."

"Well . . ."

"Maybe between the two of us, we can keep me from burning our breakfast. Don't worry about the rolls, Greta made them and gave me enough to get us through the next couple of days."

He raised his cup and grinned. "Call me Simeon." He wasn't as good-looking as Jack, and from what Sam had told her, he was a kind, caring man. She felt safe with him. His wife was a lucky woman.

AFTER LUNCH AND A FEW more hours on the trail, Sarah was ready to jump down from the wagon seat where she and Tommy had been bouncing since eating. Both her back and rear end were sore, and she was sure a few teeth were loose from her jaws snapping together.

Rose and Tulip had picked up speed. They must have sensed they were heading home, or maybe it was because there were no other wagons to slow them down. Either way, she had no idea they could move so fast.

"Are we going back to Mr. Bard, Mommy?"

Sarah's heart ached. Jack had made quite an impression on her son. She'd have to be careful in the future to not let Tommy get close to another man until she knew he was the one to marry.

"No, honey. We're going to Fort Laramie, then home to Independence."

"Why not?"

Holding back a sigh, she wrapped her arm around Tommy's shoulders. She'd lost track of the times he'd asked about Jack. She had no idea how to explain anymore. "Because he needed to go to his home.

"But why . . ."

A shot rang out interrupting Tommy's incessant questions. Had Simeon shot an antelope? His empty horse galloped past.

Sarah jerked on the reins. The wagon slowed. Where was Simeon? Were they being attacked? A familiar odor hit her nose. Her breath froze as Horace rode up beside them and stopped. Her stomach rolled at his leer.

"Well, well, well. Lookee who we have here."

Bile rose in Sarah's throat. "What are you doing here, Mr. Manny? You're supposed to be locked up at Fort Laramie." Sarah pushed Tommy. "Get in the wagon and hide," she whispered to Tommy. "Don't come out no matter what."

She searched around for her guide. "Where's Mr. Willis?"

"He's fine. Just nicked him." Horace's smile sent shivers down her spine. If she ever saw evil again, it would look exactly like the man staring down at her from the top of his horse.

Horace leaned one elbow on the pommel and held up the other, handcuffs dangling from his wrist. "It appears the army needs to do a better job of chaining up innocent men."

His spit hit the edge of her skirt.

Sarah scooted to the other side of the wagon bench. If she moved any further away, she'd fall off. Simeon's unmoving legs appeared at the edge of the wagon.

"You killed him, you bastard."

Horace shook his head. "Is that any way for a lady to talk?"

Maybe if she kept up the bravado, he'd leave her alone. Beneath the folds of her skirt, she inched her hand toward the rifle hooked on the side of the seat. "It is when I'm talking to a bastard."

"I didn't kill him, my dear Sarah. If'n you keep talkin' like that, I will. No woman of mine will call me a bastard."

She touched the butt of the rifle. "As I've told you before, I am not nor will I ever be your woman."

Horace siddled his horse close enough to grab her arm and drag her across the seat. The movement jerked her hand away from the rifle. Even if she was at his mercy, she wasn't going to give in without a fight. Damn. Why hadn't she thought to put her small gun into her skirt pocket this morning?

"Now, here's the thing. I don't see your lover, Billabard here to help you. I kinda wonder why he deserted you."

After dismounting, he yanked her from the wagon and dropped her to the ground. She stumbled and fell.

"That's what I like to see, a woman on her knees before me. Women are here to serve men, and I plan on making you serve me over and over and over again." His sneer deepened. "I saw what you gave Billabard. Kissing and carrying on. I expect the same."

Had he seen them kissing the night of the dance? Or even worse, making love under the tree? The thought of this horrible man watching them in intimate moments sickened her.

He roughly hauled her to her feet and against his body. She held back a gag at his smell. Bile rose to her throat when he pressed his lips against hers.

"Your mine now, b . . ." He jumped back and wiped her breakfast and lunch from his face. "What the hell."

"That's how I feel about you, Manny. You make me throw up. You're a disgusting excuse for a man."

Before she had a chance to react, he drew back his hand and hit her in the side of the face, toppling her sideways into the wheel.

"Tommy, stay where you are," she managed to yell as lights flashed behind her eyes and her world went dark.

SARAH'S BRAIN POUNDED in her head. Her face stung and wrists burned. Why would her wrists burn? She opened her eyes. A tight rope was wound around both wrists and to the pommel of a saddle. The sky was dark. A scent so vile she nearly threw up again, blew across her nostrils. She was tied up in front of Horace. His arms curved around her body, hands resting on her thighs.

"Where are we?"

"So, the lady is awake now. We're halfway between here and there, my love."

She listened. No sounds of oxen hoofs, creaking wheels, or clanging pots. Oh, my God. Where was her wagon? What had he done with Tommy and Simeon?

"You bastard." She clenched her teeth to keep from screaming. "Where's Tommy? If you've harmed one hair on my son's head I'll kill you."

"Don't worry, my sweet," he whispered into her ear. Gripping her thighs tighter, he tugged her bottom back against his semi-erect groin. "I didn't do anything to him."

Sarah forced back a shudder. "Then where is he? I want my son."

"Which isn't going to happen, my dear. When your friend came to, I tied him to the seat of the wagon and set the oxen moving. He should be on his way to Fort Laramie."

"What about Tommy?"

"It appears your son knows how to listen to his mother. No matter how much I tried to convince the brat I wouldn't hurt him, he stayed hidden. So, he's still hiding in the wagon." Horace shrugged against her back. "I don't care. As long as the brat is out of the way."

Sarah wouldn't give the satisfaction of breathing a sigh of relief or showing fear. Controlling her rolling stomach and pounding heart was difficult. There was no telling what he'd do if she threw up on him again. She worked the ropes with damp fingers. If she could get them loose, maybe she could jump from the horse and run away. The problem was, it was dark, and she had no idea where they were. It looked as if Horace had won—for now.

Chapter Fourteen

Jack leaned against the large boulder and stared at the river's rushing water. It had been four days, he checked his pocket watch, seven hours and twenty-three minutes since he'd ridden away from Sarah and Tommy. Not that he was counting.

Papaya nickered. He hadn't been back to this place in the mountains since the day he'd buried Lily. Once he'd left Fort Laramie with supplies and returned to the worn-looking cabin, something had compelled him to head back up here.

A piece of jerky lodged in his throat and tears trickled down his cheeks. He was weary in body and soul. He missed Lily. Most of all he missed Sarah and Tommy. How could he keep his promise and be falling in love with Sarah?

Like the day four years ago, he pulled his hat over his eyes as they drooped closed and slumber took over.

FULL, ENTICING LIPS swept over his. Warm, sultry breath blew across his face. Breath smelling like sunshine and grass. Grass? What the hell?

"Dammit, Papaya," he pushed at his horse's head, "go away. Let me sleep."

Papaya nudged and prodded until Jack nearly fell over. It wasn't as cold as the day years ago. The air was hazy when he peeled one gritty eye open. He rubbed both sides of his face trying to wake up, then stood and stretched the kinks from his body.

Papaya tugged at his sleeve and pulled him away from the rock. "Dammit, horse, leave me alone." He pushed the horse to the side. The sun rising behind the mountains from the east cast a shadow on a tree. He pushed his hat to the back of his head and scratched his scalp.

"Well, I'll be damned." Was this another dream? "Ouch!" He swatted at Papaya. "Dammit, horse, stop biting me." Jack rubbed his aching ear. "Wait. If I can feel this, then the tree can't be a dream." He peered through the mist. There was the same twisted and gnarled trunk. The same rough bark and silvery, shimmering leaves. The same silent call to beckon him closer.

He dipped beneath its branches. His hand shook as he reached out to touch the trunk. The instant he came in contact, his fingers tingled. Then his arm. He tried to pull away but couldn't move.

Warmth spread through his body then settled in his aching heart. Was he hallucinating or was the tree humming? His heart calmed, then sped up. Would the woman and boy appear again?

Between the hanging branches a person, surrounded by a foggy haze, appeared. A small boy and a woman swung hands as if they didn't have a care in the world. The woman's bonnet hung down her back, loose blonde hair flowing to her waist.

The woman looked over her shoulder and smiled. Jack's breath caught. Sarah and Tommy? Was this what the tree had been telling him before? Sarah and Tommy were his future? Is that why the tree appeared to Sarah and him on the trail?

The vision wavered like a sea of tall prairie grass blowing in the wind. Sarah and Tommy faded away. "Wait." He raced toward the empty space. A new vision appeared, one making his heart lurch.

Sarah's wagon was stopped. A man lay still on the ground beside it. The back of Sarah's head appeared to the side of the canvas, then jerked away.

The scene wavered again. Sarah was now tied to the pommel of a saddle. Tears ran down her face. A man riding behind her whispered into her ear. Jack squinted his eyes to get a better view.

Shit. Horace. The scene grew faint.

"Wait. Where is she?"

He rushed to the tree and shook a branch. "Tell me where she is," he yelled between clenched teeth. "Tell me how to find her."

"Your heart will know," the tree whispered and vanished.

Damn it. He grabbed Papaya's blanket and saddle. What the hell did the tree mean, 'your heart will know?' When he had his horse ready, Jack swung onto the saddle.

Papaya must have sensed Jack's urgency. The instant he was seated and without any urging, the horse took off down the mountain. Jack cursed under his breath each time they slowed to weave their way through rocks. As soon as they had an open space, Papaya took off in a full gallop.

How did Horace get away? Had the judge decided he was innocent? Had he escaped? How had he found Sarah? Where was Tommy? The questions pounded his brain as hard as Papaya's hooves pounded the turf.

In record time, his cabin came into view. His feet hit the ground before the horse came to a complete stop. There was no time to waste. Papaya's sides heaved. He needed to switch horses. Once he was in the barn, Jack removed the stallion's saddle, damp blanket, and bridle.

He yanked a dry blanket from a stall wall and tossed it over Jewel's back. As he lifted the saddle, Papaya nudged him to the side.

"Dammit, Papaya, I'm in a hurry. I have to find Sarah and Tommy." Jack swung the saddle again, and again Papaya prodded him, only this time harder, nearly knocking Jack over.

He caught himself on the wall before toppling over. "What the hell is wrong with you?

Papaya tossed his head up and down and nickered. He took Jewel's blanket between his teeth, pulled it from her back, then flipped it over his head.

Jack shook his head. At this rate he was never going to leave. He reached for the blanket then stopped. "Well, I'll be. You want to go with me. Right, old boy?" He grinned at Papaya's nod then straightened the blanket. "If you think you can go on, then let's get going."

In a matter of minutes, they were back on the trail heading to a place he figured would hold some answers—Fort Laramie. Since Papaya knew the trail, he let the horse take the lead and let his mind wander to Sarah.

How could he have left them? He should have known Manny would find a way to get loose and find her. His stomach knotted with guilt. Sarah's words came back to him. 'Sometimes guilt is a way of handling events that are out of our control.' She was right.

How was he to know Manny would somehow get out of jail? Had he known, he wouldn't have left Sarah and Tommy. Or would he? For the past four years, he done nothing but survive and keep his promise to Lily.

Jack gripped the reins tighter. Papaya's body flexed for a leap over a downed tree trunk lying across the trail. Good thing he and his horse knew each other so well and he could sense Papaya's next move or he'd be flying through the air.

Papaya landed safely and continued at a breakneck pace. Jack resumed his thoughts about Sarah. The woman was not only beautiful, but she was also kind, smart, strong, and wise. And even though she loved him, Lily never responded with such abandon during sex the way Sarah had.

He was a fool to leave her for a promise made to his wife. Didn't he deserve to go on with his life? Find love? Marry and have more children?

What exactly had been his promise anyway? He thought for a few seconds. It wasn't that he wouldn't find another, but that there would be no other like Lily. Which was true. There was only one Lily, and only one Sarah. One woman could not replace the other, only make a new life with him.

Why had it taken him so long to figure this out? There had been plenty of women over the years who wished to share their lives with him. Women whom he ignored in honor of his memories of Lily. Ignored his physical needs as well as his emotional.

Why now? Why Sarah? Would loving Sarah lessen his love and memories of Lily? The simple answer was no. Hopefully he wouldn't be too late to save Sarah and their love.

As Papaya slowed for a rocky stream, picking his way across the slippery stones, the tree's words came back to him. 'Your heart will know.' Then he understood. He was leaving one love behind and riding to another. There was only one place where both would meet.

With renewed vigor, once on the other side of the stream, he slapped the reins against Papaya's flank. "C'mon, boy. We've got a family to save."

Chapter Fifteen

It was now or never. Laying on her side Sarah struggled against the ropes cutting into her wrists. Her shoulders ached from her arms being forced behind her back all night. Her toes were cold and fingers numb. Even though daylight crept over the mountain tops, sending off a pink glow to the air, it would be a while before the sun crested their peaks and warmed the air.

Horace was curled up several feet away, a blanket wrapped around his head and shoulders, snoring. She shivered in the cool morning air. Her dress was damp from being on the ground all night. Of course, a *gentleman* like Horace would never offer his blanket to a lady. She'd never have put the disgusting cover near her anyway. Her stomach rumbled. He hadn't offered any of his food, either.

Sarah rolled to her knees and wiggled her hands. She wasn't sure what time they'd stopped last night. In his rush to eat a cold meal of hardtack and dried beef, he'd untied the rope, yanked her from the horse, and re-tied her hands behind her back, but not before he'd squeezed her breasts.

"These'll be mine soon, little lady. Once I get rested up, we'll have us a little fun. I'll make you forget Billabard."

When Sarah spit in his face, she was rewarded with a slap across the cheek. "I'd rather die than have your grubby hands on me." Jackass probably didn't expect a woman to fight back. Well, he was in for a surprise. She moved her jaw back and forth. No permanent damage, though. There would probably be a bruise.

If only he'd left her hands in front of her, she could use her teeth to release them. Keeping her eyes on the disgusting man, she worked her thumbs outside the ropes. Once they were free, there was enough slack to twist her hands over and over until the rope dropped to the ground.

Rubbing her wrists and shoulders, she rose, keeping as quiet as possible. She took one step backward, then another until she reached a large boulder. Horace's snores continued in an irritating cadence. At least they covered her footsteps. His horse was nowhere to be seen. Had it run off? She wouldn't blame the poor thing. Horace had ridden her hard yesterday.

Once on the other side of the boulder, she took off her skirt and petticoat. Having had the entire night to formulate a plan, she knew running in a long skirt would be difficult. At this point she didn't give a damn if someone saw her in her bloomers. As long as they came to her aide.

The air chilled her bare calves as she rolled her garments into a bundle. It would be quieter if she took off her boots, too. But with the rocks and prickly pear dotting the ground, she was better off leaving them on.

Sarah skittered from boulder to boulder, checking her distance from Horace each time. When he was no longer in sight, she picked up speed and raced east, hopefully toward Fort Laramie, praying the entire time that Horace was still sleeping and Tommy safe.

How long had she run? A stitch in her side made her stop. Her mouth was dry, her legs and lungs burned from unaccustomed running, and her stomach growled. Perspiration ran down her face and into her eyes. She'd snagged her bonnet on a bush and hadn't taken the time to retrieve it.

How far had she come? Hopefully far enough so Horace couldn't catch up with her any time soon—unless he'd found his horse. Then she'd be in trouble.

The pain in her side subsided long enough to keep going. In the distance a plume of smoke spiraled to the sky. Fort Laramie? Would she find Tommy there? She cupped her eyes against the morning sun now fully above the mountains. A stand of trees stood between her and the smoke. How far was it? Half a mile? A mile? Distance in this vast land was difficult to determine. It didn't matter, she needed to continue and find her son.

With her eyes on the smoke and trees, she ran.

WATER. SHE NEEDED WATER. Sarah leaned on a wooden fence surrounding a half dozen crudely carved wooden crosses and as many headstones fashioned from rock. Names, year of birth and death, and in some cases, a prayer or something about the deceased were etched in the stones. She climbed over the fence and wove her way through the crosses and headstones until one caught her eye.

The tallest in the cemetery, it was as if someone wanted everyone to know the importance of the deceased. Sarah stopped.

Here lies Lily Mae Billabard and her infant son, James. Beloved wife of Jack Billabard. There will never be another like you. Born, 1835 Died 1855 Rest in Peace, My Love

Poor Jack and his promise to Lily. She continued to harbor hope he'd come back to her. After reading this, she knew there was no chance. He was still in love with his wife. A wife who could no longer give him the warmth, comfort, and love she could.

Sarah ducked behind the headstone when a shout came from the west and another from the east. Both called her name. Both rode horses, coming closer and closer. One held anger. The other, she hoped, held love. She curled into a tight ball.

"Sarah Nickelson, you come out here right now. We have business to finish." Horace was definitely the angry one. His footsteps crunched on the ground, coming closer and closer. He fisted her hair and yanked her to her feet.

"Ouch. Let go of me." She slapped at his hand, then kicked him in the shin. Grabbing her leg, he dropped her to the ground.

"You're going to pay for this, witch." He lifted his arm, hand clenched in a fist.

She ducked, covering her head with her arms and braced for the blow.

"Hit her and you're a dead man."

Sarah peered from beneath her arms. A man pointed a rifle at Horace. Even with the sun behind him, Jack's silhouette was unmistakable.

Relief rushed through to be replaced by fear when the distinctive sound of a gun slipping from a holster and the hammer clicking back echoed in the air.

"Put the rifle down, Billabard, or I'll shoot her." Horace jerked Sarah up by her hair, wrapped his free hand around her throat, and put the gun to her temple.

"You going to hide behind a simple woman, Manny?"

Simple? Did Jack just call her simple? She narrowed her eyes at him. She'd tell him who was simple. His wink was so slight, she almost missed it. He was egging Horace on.

"Please, Jack. Put the gun down." Hopefully, her attempt as a helpless female would fool Horace. "Poor Mr. Manny can't help it he can't fight for me himself. Let him hide behind me. Some men aren't man enough and need a woman to guide him."

Horace's hold on her throat tightened, nearly cutting off her air. "Are you calling me a coward, woman?"

Sarah kept her eyes on Jack's face. With Horace looking down at her, he couldn't see his nod of approval.

Sarah dug her nails into Horace's arm. "Yes. You're a coward."

With a low growl, Horace tossed her to the side. "No one calls me a coward. Not Billabard and certainly not a woman."

Jack kept his rifle trained on Horace. "Then how about we settle this like men. No guns. No knives. Just you, me, and fists."

Sarah had no doubt Jack had the advantage. He was younger, taller, and more muscular. Horace had rage on his side, and if smells could kill, she would have been dead already.

"Sarah, come here and take the rifle. Keep it pointed on Manny." Jack's hard stare took in her state of undress. "Where are your clothes, honey? Did he hurt you?"

Thankfully, the anger in his eyes wasn't aimed at her. "No. I got away while he was sleeping. I don't know where Tommy is."

The muscles in Jack's jaw didn't relax as he handed her the rifle. "His abducting you is bad enough. Shoot him if he tries anything funny."

Horace laughed. "She wouldn't shoot me."

"Want to take a bet, Mr. Manny?" She glared at him down the barrel of the rifle, taking aim at his heart. Horace's Adam's apple bobbed up and down. "Did I or did I not take lessons on using guns before I joined the wagon train? Was I or was I not able to shoot down nine out of ten cans from a fence?"

She lowered the gun toward his crotch. "Are you willing to take the chance? Put down your gun."

Horace's face paled. He placed the gun on the ground.

"Now the knives I know you have hidden in both your boots."

"What about him?" Horace nodded his chin at Jack.

"Jack, you got any other weapons? Let's make this fair and square. I wouldn't want this coward to say you cheated."

The skunk had the nerve to laugh. "You have a lot of confidence in him, don't you?"

"Of course I do. He's not a coward."

With bared teeth, Horace removed two long, sharp-edged knives from his boots and put them next to his gun. He took off his long coat, revealing a sweat-stained shirt.

Jack slid off his buckskin jacket, laid it over Lily's headstone, then raised his hands, palm side up. "I don't have any other weapons."

"Move back, Mr. Manny." Sarah signaled with the rifle. Once he was safely away from his weapons, she picked up the gun, and after emptying the chamber, laid it on top of Jack's coat. At Jack's raised eyebrow, she said, "I did take lessons." Keeping an eye on the men, Sarah put on her skirt, leaving the petticoat on the ground.

Knees bent, arms outstretched, the men circled each other several times before Horace charged, knocking Jack into a tree.

Jack grabbed a low branch and swung up, kicking his legs out and into Horace's stomach. Horace landed on his back. In a movement Sarah didn't think he was capable of, he jumped to his feet.

Uniformed men appeared around the perimeter of the cemetery. A man with several stripes on his sleeves stood beside her and took the rifle. "I'm Sergeant Willows, ma'am. Weren't you here a few days ago with Sam's outfit?"

Sarah nodded and held back a scream when Horace planted his fist on Jack's jaw. He staggered back, then regained his balance. When Horace charged, his head down, Jack stepped aside. Manny hugged the air before landing on his knees.

"Isn't that Horace Manny?" Willow asked. "We've been trying to find him."

Sarah swung her fists in the air, like she was hitting a phantom opponent. "C'mon, Jack. Let him have it."

Willow unloaded the rifle and set the butt on the toe of his boot. "What's Manny doing here?"

"I was heading to the fort with my son and guide. Manny shot my guide and left him and my son behind when Manny abducted me. I got away and found my way here. Manny followed, and Jack is giving the skunk a beating he deserves."

After a shove from Manny, Jack landed at Sarah's feet. A grin split his face as he stared up at her. "I love you, Sarah Nickelson."

Before she could respond. Horace grabbed Jack's shirt front and yanked him to his feet. Sarah cupped her hands around her mouth. "I know."

Jack's next swing sent Horace to his knees. A kick to his face toppled him to his back. He stood over Horace, his chest heaving, breath wheezing. He bent at the waist and rested his palms on his knees. "Give up, Manny?"

Horace looked up at him and nodded. Only then did Jack walk toward Sarah. Blood dribbled from a cut in the corner of his lip. One red eye was half closed. His knuckles were scraped and torn, and his shirt ripped in half. He'd done this for her. He'd said he loved her.

Sarah's heart swelled with love. In the next instant she screamed. "Jack, behind you."

Screaming profanities, Horace charged across the cemetery toward them. Before he reached Jack, he tripped on a tree root and fell forward. A crack rent the air and Horace lay still.

With his gun poised, Willow approached the fallen man. "C'mon, Manny. Get up so I can haul your ass back to the stockade." Horace didn't move. The sergeant motioned to two men to roll Horace over.

Sarah's stomach heaved. Strong arms wrapped around her. She buried her face in Jack's chest. The vision of Horace's bloody, smashed face would forever be in her mind. Blood trickled from his nose and lips. While one sightless eye remained open, the other, bruised and swollen, was closed.

Willow shook his head. "It appears he landed on this headstone and broke his neck."

Jack cupped the back of Sarah's head. "C'mon, let's go to the fort."

Sarah clutched the front of his shirt. "We need to find Tommy." She held back the sob building in her chest. "I need my son."

"We'll find him, Sarah. We'll get you a horse at the fort and head out right away."

"Don't worry, Mrs. Nickelson," Willow said, motioning to his men to cover Horace. "I have men looking for them right now."

A soldier marched up to Willow and whispered in his ear. Willow nodded, faced Sarah, and grinned. "Some of my men found them a few miles away. They'll be at the fort shortly."

Chapter Sixteen

Jack jerked back his head as Sarah dabbed at the blood on his lips and a cut at the corner of his eye. After several soldiers hauled Horace's body to the edge of the cemetery to be interred, they were taken to a room at Fort Laramie.

"Don't be such a baby, Jack."

"Huh. You call beating up that skunk being a baby?"

"Of course not. You're my hero." She kissed the corner of his mouth and stepped back. Even though Jack was with her, she was worried sick about Tommy. "Where is he? Why aren't they back here yet? Do you think something has happened to him?"

His movements stiff, he stood. "I'm sure he's fine. Remember how stubborn your oxen can be?"

Sarah worried her bottom lip and nodded. "Blasted beasts. Yesterday they were in such a hurry." Jack's embrace calmed her ragged nerves.

"It'll be all right. If something was wrong, they'd tell us." He kissed her temple. "If he doesn't get here in the next hour, we'll go out ourselves."

Sarah stepped back and stood behind one of the chairs. Even bruised, he was the most handsome man she'd ever seen. How did she get so lucky to find a man like Jack Billabard? Had he said he loved her in the heat of the moment or had he really meant it?

She was no longer the shy woman from Independence who let a man tell her what to do. She'd learned to drive a team of oxen, fix her wagon, and cook over a fire. Well, maybe the h one was a stretch. She'd made new friends and managed to get away from Horace. So, if she couldn't tell a man she loved him, then she was a coward. She took a deep breath and rested her hands on the back of a chair. "I love you, Jack."

His one good eye glimmered. "I . . ."

The door opened. "Mrs. Nickelson," Willow said, "we have a little problem."

A jolt of fear slammed through her. She gripped Jack's hand. "Oh, my God. Tommy. What happened to my son?"

"He's fine. Evidently you told him not to leave the wagon, and he's taken you at your word. Nothing we do or say will get him to leave." Willow smiled. "One of my men tried climbing in through the back. Your dog bit him on the arm. Another tried through the front, but a man inside pulled a gun on us."

Sarah didn't care what happened to the soldiers, she just wanted to get to Tommy. To her dismay, instead of taking her to him, Willow went on.

"We decided to haul the whole thing back to the fort, lock, stock, boy, growling dog, squalling puppies, and man."

Sarah couldn't stand it anymore. "Sergeant Willow, I appreciate everything you've done, but could you please take me to my son."

SARAH SHADED HER EYES with her hand against the glaring sun in the yard. Her heart skipped a beat. Joy bubbled through her chest. There stood her wagon, Rose and Tulip attached in the front, George tied to the rear, bellowing to be milked.

Several soldiers milled about, a couple muttering about 'those damn oxen,' 'that blasted dog,' and 'a brave boy.' Simeon Willis sat on the ground being attended by the fort's doctor.

Lifting her skirt, she raced to the wagon, Jack right behind her. With his hands at her waist, he lifted her to the seat.

"Tommy?" Sarah leaned into the dim interior. "Tommy, honey. It's Mommy. You can come out now."

In a blur, a small body jumped into her arms.

"Mommy. Mommy. I founded you. I founded you."

Peace settled in her soul as his small arms wrapped around her neck. Tommy kissed her cheeks.

"I stayed hidden like you told me to. I gots hungry, though, so I ate some apples." He leaned back in her arms, a frown on his face. "You won't be mad at me for eating them without asking, will you?"

Sarah laughed for the pure joy of having her son back in her arms. "No, I won't be mad at you." She didn't think she'd ever let him go.

He kissed her cheek again, then wiggled from her arms. She wanted to protest the loss of his small arms around his neck when he squealed.

"Mr. Bard, Mr. Bard. You're back." Tommy jumped into his arms.

Jack groaned and held Tommy against his chest. "Tommy, be careful, Mr. Billabard is hurt."

"How did you get hurt, Mr. Bard?"

"He got hurt saving me from Mr. Manny. He's a hero."

With one arm still holding Tommy, he slung his other one over her shoulders. "You're a hero, too, Mrs. Nickelson." His lips caressed her cheek. "Let's tell our stories later. Right now, there's something we need to do before heading to my place."

Sarah frowned. Had she heard right? They were going to his place? "What is it?"

"You'll see." With a lop-sided grin and a hitching gait, he led them from the room.

Chapter Seventeen

As her wagon pitched and bumped over the trail to Jack's cabin, Sarah held out her left hand. She was now Mrs. Jack Billabard. She should probably be upset about the heavy-handed way he had taken charge. In a matter of minutes, he'd located the Army's chaplain and explained what he wanted.

As word spread there was to be a wedding, the few women in the fort took over. A tub was brought into the major's office and filled with steaming water. While she luxuriated in cleaning days of dirt and Horace's stench from her, several women went to her wagon and located the dress she'd made for her wedding to Mr. Sampson. Once she was clean and patted dry, the women slid the dress over her head and arranged her hair to fit beneath the matching hat.

Gazing longingly at the matching parasol, Sarah accepted a bouquet of wildflowers tied with a satin purple ribbon. With all the work the women had done for her, she didn't have the heart to reject their offering.

With a few sniffles in the background, Sarah repeated her vows to a clean, dashing Jack. His hair, still wet from his bath, was slicked back from his forehead with one errant piece drooping down to his left eye. He wore a flannel shirt tucked into dark blue pants he must have borrowed from someone several inches shorter than him. Who was she to complain? After all, he hadn't come to the fort for a wedding. Besides, she would have married him in his long johns.

Someone had cleaned up Tommy. His beaming face shone like polish had been taken to it. His pants, also too short, were clean and held up by suspenders which for once weren't twisted. He slipped one small hand into Sarah's and one into Jack's, holding them both while they faced each other to repeat their vows. With Jack holding her other hand, they formed a perfect circle. A circle of love.

If Jack's words were a little slurred and their kiss just a brief touching of his swollen lips to hers, Sarah didn't mind. There'd be years to make up for it.

Now they were on their way to Jack's, no their home. The major, married with a son Tommy's age, had convinced them to leave Tommy behind for a few days.

"After all," he'd said with a wink, "a marriage shouldn't start with a six-year-old underfoot."

She was torn between never leaving her son again and being with her new husband. Since Tommy was already off playing with the other children, and it was only for a few days, she relented.

Jack set the wagon's brake in front of the cabin, eased himself down, and came to her side.

"I'd love to help you down, but I'm afraid I'd drop you."

"Don't worry, I've done this a few times." She looked at the train of her skirt. "Never in a dress this fancy, though."

JACK LOOKED AT THE material flowing down the back of her dress. Even though she'd looked as beautiful as a sunset over the mountains, the dress was impractical for a ranch. It would probably be stored and only brought out when one of their daughters got married.

His blood quickened. Daughters and sons. Hopefully, they'll have a passel of them.

With the grace of an antelope, Sarah got down from her perch. Worried about what she'd think when she saw the inside of a cabin that had been pretty much ignored over the past years, he was pleasantly surprised. With the dress's train slung over her arm, she walked around the kitchen and living area, poked her head into his room, then a room that would be perfect for Tommy. Once they had children of their own, they'd have to add on. Maybe upward.

"This is so big. And bright." She wrinkled her nose. "With a little cleaning, this will be perfect."

Damn his aching body. Thankfully, his ribs weren't broken, only bruised. Even if they had been, there was no way he wouldn't make love to his new wife. Hell, with his puffed-up eye, he could only see half of her. He'd just have to use his good eye to view every inch of her.

"Uh, Sarah?"

She stopped checking out the cast-iron stove and smiled at him over her shoulder. "Yes?"

"I'd like to take you to a special place." He took in her fancy dress again. "You'll have to change into something a little less dressy."

"I know just the thing. It'll take only a moment to get what I need."

The few minutes she was gone seemed like an eternity. Was she changing in the wagon?

"Will this do?" Sarah held up a blouse and a skirt. She turned her back to him. "If you'll unbutton me."

Jack cussed at his shaking fingers as he released each one of the many buttons going down her back. As each button was opened, more of her skin was exposed. Her long, elegant neck and white, smooth shoulders. Her delicate upper back. Since he hadn't seen her completely naked before, he'd had to use his imagination to visualize what was hidden beneath her chemise. Her back tapered to a small waist. His fingers burned at the last button at the top of her ass.

Even if it meant torturing himself, he needed to see if his imagination lived up to the real thing. He slid the dress down her shoulders, her arms, to her waist, to the floor, the satin whispering in the silence of the room.

He turned her to face him and untied her petticoat, letting it drop on top of her dress. With trembling hands, he undid the top ribbon of her chemise, then the succeeding two. The material draped down her perfect, soft, white breasts. Reality was so much better than his imagination.

He burned to taste her rosy nipples again and ran a finger from the top of her left breast and over her nipple, making it pucker.

Her breath hitched. "That feels wonderful. Please don't stop."

His cock twitched. Not here. He wanted their first night together to be where the tree had first shown her to him. "As much as I want you now, there's somewhere I want to take you."

Sarah cupped his face as gently as she would a newborn babe. Her kisses were as light as the wind yet carried a punch going clear down to his privates.

"I'm going to get dressed so you can take me to this special place of yours."

Drawing his eyes from her perfect body, Jack put food in his saddlebag and readied a bedroll. He unhitched Papaya from the back of Sarah's wagon and led Jewel from the barn. Thankfully, someone had brushed, fed, and re-saddled his horse at Fort Laramie. All he needed to do was take care of Jewel.

Jack nearly lost his ability to speak, when Sarah appeared wearing a simple white, over-the-shoulder blouse tucked into a dark blue, split skirt. The scooped, gathered edge of the top exposed her chest. Dark nipples pebbled beneath the fabric. Wasn't she wearing anything beneath it?

He swallowed around the lump in his throat. "What are you wearing?"

"Don't you like it?" she asked, picking up Jewel's saddle.

"Hell, Sarah. I love it. So much so, that we may not leave here until I have my way with you."

Her grin over her shoulder went straight to his groin. "Would that be so bad?"

"I'd rather have our first time as husband and wife not in a stuffy, dirty house, but out in the open." He paused, watching her struggle with getting the saddle over Jewel's back. "What are you doing?"

"Saddling what I assume is my horse." She tightened the belt beneath Jewel's belly.

"That's my job. What kind of man do you think I am that I'd let my wife saddle her own horse?"

"The kind of man who is sore from rescuing his woman." With the reins in her hands, she leaned against the hitching post and crossed her arms over her chest.

Worry settled in his gut when she didn't look at him. Was she going to tell him the marriage was over before it even began?

"I don't know what kind of life you had with Lily, but I don't want what I had with Peter. If I were hurt or sick, would you cook for me?"

"Of course I would."

"When we have children, would you leave me to raise them by myself?"

Where was she going with this? "Good heavens. No."

"Then why would I expect you to handle things by yourself? You're sore from the fight with Manny. Your pain is my pain. Your work is my work, just as my pain and work should be yours."

Jack's heart filled. What had he done to deserve a second chance at love? He put his hands on her shoulders and cupped her face as she had done earlier. "I think I'm going to love being your husband."

FOR THE FIRST TIME in years, the ride to his mountain was slow and peaceful. Gone was the anger and guilt dogging him in the past. Except for the pain in his cock from watching Sarah's breasts sway with the movements of her horse, there was a calm, heart-warming sense of place.

He laughed at her stories of Tommy's antics. He shared his growing up with a bunch of rowdy brothers and sisters. They were getting to know one another, and as time passed, he fell for her more and more.

"We're here." Jack halted Papaya near the boulder, held the pommel, and swung from the saddle.

"It's absolutely breathtaking." She took a deep breath and dismounted. "And smells heavenly."

He'd always loved the scent of pine trees, the river, and fresh, crisp air. Now that he knew Sarah loved it, too, it would be even more special. They'd have to make a point of coming up here often.

He left Sarah watching a pair of otters playing in the river, made a soft bed of pine needles where the tree first appeared, and spread out his bedroll. Once he was satisfied it would be comfortable, he stood behind her and put his hands on her shoulders.

"As much fun as it is watching those otters, I can think of something more fun to do."

Sarah turned in his arms. "And what would that be, husband?"

"Seeing you completely naked." Her top made it easy to slide the sleeves down her shoulders until her breasts came into view. Lower and lower until her nipples were visible. His entire body shuddered with wanting Sarah. "Beautiful. Absolutely beautiful."

EVEN THOUGH SARAH KNEW she wasn't beautiful, his words made her feel like the most gorgeous woman in the world. Sparks shot through her as he slid her top down her arms until she was exposed from the waist up.

She swore steam rose from her heated skin as he peppered kisses on her neck, her shoulders, and chest. She drew in a deep breath when he sucked one nipple, then the other. He unbuttoned her skirt and let it drop to the ground leaving her naked except for her boots.

Jack cupped her ass and pressed it against his crotch.

She needed to feel his bare skin against her. Feel the heat of his body, the hardness of his penis. "There's something wrong with this picture."

"What?" Jack's deep voice quivered.

"You're dressed."

Without taking his eyes from her, he tore off his clothes and stood before her in all his naked glory. In daylight she saw what darkness had hidden before. Broad shoulders. Muscled chest covered with dark hair leading down to slim hips and . . . Oh, goodness. . . His hard cock bouncing against his stomach. Her muscles clenched knowing where his cock would end up. She didn't know how long she could wait.

Jack swooped her up and carried her to their makeshift bed and laid her down as if she was the most precious piece of glass. He removed their boots.

"*Completely* naked," he said, laying on top of her. His cock pressed against her stomach. "Even though I want to kiss every inch of you, I'm not sure how long I can wait, Sarah."

Sarah welcomed his weight and his words. "I've been wanting you since our first time together." She skimmed her hands down his muscled back and shoulders, then his tight ass, pulling him closer. She didn't know a man's skin could be so soft. "And even before that."

"Thank goodness," he mumbled against her right breast, flicking his tongue across the tip, then sucking the nipple of her left breast deeply into his mouth until she was squirming with need.

With a groan, he released her breast and took her mouth, capturing her tongue with his own as he slowly buried his cock into her. Deepening their kiss, he set up a driving pace, rocking her world with the force of her pleasure.

Sarah wrapped her legs around his waist and matched his movements, thrust after thrust. As a powerful pressure built inside her, she thought she'd die from the exquisite feeling, until the flames he'd awakened in her exploded into a fireball.

Jack moaned and with one last thrust, the warmth of his seed filled her.

AFTER A FEW MOMENTS, Jack touched his forehead to hers.

"I love you, Sarah Billabard."

"I love you, too. Jack Billabard."

From the corner of his eye, he noticed something shimmering. "It's back." He rolled away from her and sat up. "The tree. Like the last time."

Sarah reached out and fingered one of the branches. "How many times have you seen it?"

"Four. The first time was after Lily died. I came up here hurt, angry, feeling guilty. The tree appeared and with it a vision of a woman and young boy. I thought I was dreaming." He ran his fingers through her hair, enjoying the silky strands against his skin. "When I first saw you and Tommy, I was shocked. You seemed familiar. As time went on, I couldn't handle my growing feelings for you, so I denied them."

Sarah sat and snuggled into his side, resting her head beneath his chin. Her warmth was as comforting as the tree, filling his heart with love.

"My first time a tall, handsome man, wearing a long coat, a wide-brimmed hat, carrying a rifle by his side appeared." She toyed with his chest hair. "Just the way you were when I saw you walking toward my wagon."

They sat in silence as the tree swayed and hummed around them.

The urge to see what would happen if they felt the tree at the same time grew in him with each passing moment. "Let's touch it together."

The leaves shimmered and fluttered. Jack cupped her hand in his, and they reached out. He may have imagined it, but a branch swayed toward them, as if beckoning their touch.

Like before, warmth spread through him. "Are your fingers tingling?"

Sarah nodded against him.

He tightened his arm around her shoulders. "Is your heart full to bursting?"

She sighed. "More than I ever thought possible."

As one they turned and looked between the branches. A vision appeared. Jack sucked in a breath. His heart constricted. The woman in the image was not his Sarah.

"Lily," he whispered, tears pooling in his eyes. She wore a lavender dress, the one she was married in. Her long, dark hair flowed away from her revealing high cheekbones and full lips. Her smile was the one she'd give him right after saying she loved him. A sob built in his chest.

"What did you say?"

Lily held a hand out to him. Jack rose. "It's Lily. Don't you see her?"

"I do, Jack. She's beautiful." Sarah's voice held a tinge of awe.

Why was she here? Why now when he'd found another to love? When he was happy again? Was Lily warning him away from Sarah?

He glanced from Lily to his new wife, who stood beside him. Sarah's smile as she reached out a hand to Lily was as beautiful as Lily's. What the hell was going on here?

"She's saying good-bye."

Jack turned his attention away from Sarah and back to the vision of Lily. "How do you know?"

"She told me." Sarah took his hand, squeezed his fingers, and rested her head on his shoulder.

A familiar, loving voice came to him.

"I'm happy. It's all right for you to be happy." Lily blew him a kiss. "I love you, Jack Billabard." Her words came as a whisper as she faded away.

He didn't know whether to scream, howl, or cry. Maybe all three. Before he chased after the allusive vision, another appeared.

A man and woman held hands. Her long golden hair flowed down her back. The man held a rifle at his side. A boy on the cusp of manhood stood beside him. A young girl appeared and held the woman's hand. One by one, more girls came into the scene.

Jack counted five children in all before they stopped entering the picture. Standing in a row, hands joined, they swung their arms back and forth, like they didn't have a care in the world. Finally, a small boy ran up and grabbed the man's legs. He bent down and swooped the boy into his arms. The woman, her stomach round with child, angled toward the man and kissed him.

Jack's lips tingled as if the vision had actually kissed him. His chest nearly burst with all the joy and happiness floating around in there.

"I believe that's us, Jack Billabard." Sarah's smile gave the sun a run for its money.

"I believe you're right, Sarah Billabard. I believe you're right."

And before their eyes, the family faded and the tree disappeared, leaving behind a promise of everlasting love.

The End

Thank you for reading "The Trail to Love." Please leave a message on Facebook as it helps authors. Please read on for the blurbs from some of my other books.

"The Balcony Girl"

When Julia Lindstrom and her sister, Suzanna, made the decision to move to Deadwood, South Dakota in 1879, Julia never suspected that she would meet her future husband, secretly befriend the madam of a brothel, or jump in to assist when disaster strikes the turbulent mining town. Can she survive all three?

Daniel Iverson followed the gold rush to Deadwood back when it was in its heyday, only to discover gold prospecting wasn't the life for him. Now working as a lawyer, a case falls into his lap regarding a rash of recent illnesses affecting the men visiting the town's saloons and brothels. Is it a disease or something more sinister?

Will a secret tear them apart or bring them together?

"The School Marm"

CAN A SCHOOL MARM WITH dreams of a better life, fall for a disreputable man?

Suzanna Lindstrom travels as a school marm in fledgling Deadwood. Having left her parents' struggling farm, she dreams of a better life in Deadwood with a man who's struck it rich in the gold fields. Fresh off the stagecoach, she meets Kingston Winson, who she disregards as disreputable. Is he who she thinks he is?

What lesson will she learn?

"The Proprietess"

CAN TWO DAMAGED HEARTS rise from the ashes?

For Leona Winson, life in the lawless town of Deadwood requires a woman to have an iron-clad spine. After a failed engagement, running King's Restaurant and Hotel has been the fresh start she needed, but she has gained a reputation around town for being no-nonsense, and opinionated. When the fire that consumed the town forces her to oversee the rebuilding of the establishment that she had put her heart and soul into, she discovers that there may be room for a second chance at love to rise from the ashes.

Asa Johnson had resigned himself to living the bachelor's life after the death of his wife. Content to work on King Winson's ranch and keep an eye on his son Josiah, Asa wasn't looking for love when he was tasked with rebuilding the only hotel and restaurant in Deadwood, and he never expected to find it in the sharp-tongued proprietress, and sister of his boss.

When the two are thrown together under extreme circumstances, their relationship blossoms, but will a mysterious traveler who arrived in town after the fire derail their love story before it can even begin?

"The Banker's Wife"

ALONE. ALWAYS ALONE. Alone because she'd killed him. She was a murderess, and the worst part was her remorse was the size of a flake of gold.

Married to a man she didn't choose, Bertha Woods is unprepared for her husband's cruelty turning her from a sweet, innocent girl who is happiest out on the farm, to a cold-hearted, lonely, society harridan. Always thinking of her first love, for twenty years she bears his scams, beatings, and hatred until she takes matters into her own hands.

Can she return to being the kind-hearted, happy woman she once was? Will she ever find love and happiness with the horse trainer who enters her life?

Travel back to Deadwood, South Dakota in 1879, and meet the characters who live and work with Bertha Woods, The Banker's Wife.

"The Unconventional Blacksmith"

WHEN THE IRON IS HOT, two hearts come together to forge a new beginning...

Serenity Edleman and her husband, Stephan, came to the thriving mining town of Deadwood, but life has a way of throwing unexpected curveballs. After her husband passes away, Serenity takes up the mantle of running her husband's blacksmith shop. It is a challenging journey in the male-dominated profession, but she gains recognition for her unique, designs. When an exciting opportunity comes her way, Serenity realizes she needs extra help. Can she find someone who doesn't want more than she's willing to give?

Titus "Bull" Galloway has been serving as a blacksmith in the Army for almost half his life. However, after coming across an advertisement in the newspaper, he feels a yearning for a fresh start. Bull and his apprentice journey to Deadwood to interview for the position with S. Edleman.

Working together presents its own set of obstacles. But, like steel sharpens steel, Bull and Serenity learned before you become unbreakable, you must first be broken down and forged into something solid and unbreakable. Something like a family.

"Missing My Heart"

CAN HIDDEN LOVE NOTES and money bring two people together or tear them apart?

Time: 1975. Place: Bourbonville, Kentucky

After the death of the grandmother Ellie Farrell had lived with since she was sixteen, she is tasked with the job of cleaning out the over-packed house. When Ellie begins to find love notes and money from a Bert to Randi spanning over four decades, she sets out to find out who these people are and what they have to do with her. An unexpected check for $100,000 dollars delivered to her house, ramps up the mystery – especially when death threats begin to arrive.

Patton Trullinger, an investigative reporter, comes to Chandler County to research bootleggers for a book he's contracted for. As a Vietnam veteran, he's dealing with PTSD. When he meets Ellie, he finds her mystery too good to pass up.

Who are Bert and Randi? Who is sending death threats? Will Ellie and Patton's love bloom as the mystery deepens?

"Missing Innocence"

BORN WITH A DISFIGURED right arm, Sally York longs to spread her wings and fly from her over-protective father and grandfather. Because of her antagonistic, teasing older sister, Sally stutters when nervous, making a job in the public eye impossible. Moving away from her family's horse ranch to start a flower-growing business takes everything she has – emotionally and physically. When her life becomes endangered with the arrival of unusual packages to her greenhouse, can the mysterious Nathan Moon help her, or is he the one she needs to run from?

Undercover FBI agent, Nathan Moon, is sent to discover how and where drugs are arriving in Ivy Downs County. With no plans for romance, meeting Sally sets him on his heels. His investigation takes him in a direction he wishes he didn't want to go. Is the shy, reserved, lovely Sally part of the drug ring?

Can Sally and Nathan overcome their distrust of each other and find the real culprits?

"A Photograph of Love"

TAKE AN ANGRY RANCHER. Add a burned-out nurse. Throw in some rustlers. Can Trudy and Link find their own photograph of love?

Trudy Selucas has watched too many people die. Burned out as a home hospice nurse, she realizes she needs a change. When she accepts an invitation to visit a friend in Texas, she uses her love of photography and roams the Texas countryside taking pictures to soothe her aching soul.

After his parents die, Lincoln Phister must leave college behind and his dreams of becoming a photojournalist. He spends the next ten years raising his three younger siblings and working the family ranch. Now he is frustrated with his job, cattle rustlers, and lack of a love life.

A chance encounter with a rattlesnake brings them together. Lincoln's anger nearly drives them apart. Can Trudy convince him to follow his dream while finding their own photograph of love?

"Love With a Side of Crazy"

AN ACCOUNTANT BY DAY, stripper by night. A sexy physical therapist. A crazed stalker. Will anyone survive?

To afford sending extra money to his parents to help with the care of his invalid brother, Brent Hopkins, an accountant by day, works as a male stripper at night. When a crazed fan pulls him from the stage, his injuries send him for an extended stay at a rehabilitation center. During his months at the center, mysterious angel statues and other gifts begin to appear in his room. A break-in at his apartment leaves him feeling vulnerable. Is he going crazy or does he have a stalker?

Marie Phister, a physical therapist, was at the club the night Brent is yanked to the ground and takes care of him until help arrives. Later, as his physical therapist, she doesn't let on that she is aware of his identity. As their mutual attraction grows, a stalker threatens their relationship.

Is her stalker and Brent's, one and the same? Can they solve the mystery before it's too late?

"Never With a Rich Man"

CASSIE JORDAN HAS BEEN lied to, cheated on, and passed over for a promotion. All by men. She was tired of men. She didn't need a man, and certainly not a rich man. Then she met Hogan Wynnters, and ordinary salesman - or so she thought.

Hogan Wynnters is part owner of a family business and has the kind of money Cassie despises. He's tired of women coming on to him because he's rich. He decides to never tell a woman about his financial status until she gets to know him as a person. As an undercover FBI agent, he uses his knowledge of antiquities to find the people who are bringing stolen WWII artifacts into the country. Unfortunately, the woman he's falling for is in the crosshairs of the FBI.

Can they work through their preconceived notions and find true love?

"Riding for Love"

EVE DAYTON, OWNER OF a riding ranch, rose above her childhood past and overcame the emotional damage her boyfriend caused when he married another woman. When someone starts sabotaging her ranch, Eve is desperate to find the culprit before she loses everything. Is it a coincidence or is the return of Denton Johanson tied to the mystery?

Divorced Denton Johanson returns to his hometown to help convict the embezzling controller of the family business. When he runs into Eve, he realizes his feelings for her are still strong enough to try and win her back. His fear of horses won't get in the way of his goal and decides the only way to be near her is to take riding lessons from her. Can he convince her that his love is real and he is not behind the mystery surrounding the ranch?

Eve Dayton's former boyfriend returns to town just as problems start arising at her horse riding ranch. Can she believe his declaration to be part of her life again? Will she overcome the suspicion that he is part of the problem and accept his help in catching the culprits? Find out how Denton Johanson triumphs over his fears to win back her love.

"Operation Santa"

HOW MUCH TROUBLE CAN a man get into while trying to win his estranged wife back? David is about to find out in this humorous novella.

About The Author

Tina Susedik is a multi-award-winning, multi-published author in both fiction and non-fiction. She is published in history, military, romantic mystery, erotic romance, and children's books, with forty-four books to her credit. Her books are in both print and eBook format.

She lives in northern Wisconsin with her husband of fifty-one years.

She also writes spicier romance as Anita Kidesu.

<u>Where to find Tina</u>

Website: www.tina-susedik.com[1]

Facebook: https://www.facebook.com/TinaSusedikAuthor/

---

1. http://www.tina-susedik.com

Pinterest: http://www.pinterest.com/tinasusedik/
Goodreads: https://www.goodreads.com/author/show/
1754353.Tina_Susedik
Newsletter: https://www.tina-susedik.com/contact

<u>Other Titles by Tina</u>
<u>Romantic Mysteries</u>
Riding for Love
Never With A Rich Man
A Photograph of Love
Crazy With a Side of Love
Operation Santa – a Novella
Saving Ellis – a Novella
<u>Historical</u>
The Trail to Love, An Oregon Trail Story
<u>The Darlings of Deadwood Series</u>
The Balcony Girl
The School Marm
The Proprietress
The Banker's Wife
Saving Ellis – A Novella
The Unconventional Blacksmith
<u>Fury Creek Series</u>
Missing My Heart
Missing Innocence
<u>Anthologies</u>
All I Want for Christmas is a Soul Mate
My Sexy Valentine
Sizzle in the Snow
The School Marm — Wild Deadwood Tales

Saving Ellis — Getting Wild in Deadwood
Rescuing Eliza — My Heart Belongs in Deadwood
The Pirates Ring - Hope Harbor Book 1
The Magic of the Whalehouse Tavern — Hope Harbor Book II
Finding Henrietta — Naughty and Nice – A Galena Holiday
Picturing Annabella — Lost and Found in Deadwood
Gruagh Gallagher – Hope Harbor Book III
The General – Galena Book II
Batty for Love – Taking A Chance in Deadwood

Children's Books

Uncle Bill's Farm
The Hat Peddler
Peanut and Casey on Uncle Bill's Farm

Writing as Anita Kidesu

South Seas Seduction
Surprise Me
Surprise Me Again
Double the Surprise